Women Who Live in Coffee Shops

Stella Pope Duarte

Arte Público Press
Houston, Texas

Women Who Live in Coffee Shops and Other Stories is made possible in part from grants from the city of Houston through the Houston Arts Alliance, the University of California at Irvine Chicano/Latino Literary Prize and by the Exemplar Program, a program of Americans for the Arts in Collaboration with the LarsonAllen Public Services Group, funded by the Ford Foundation.

Recovering the past, creating the future

Arte Público Press
University of Houston
452 Cullen Performance Hall
Houston, Texas 77204-2004

Cover illustration by Cristina Cardenas
Cover design by Mora Des!gn

Duarte, Stella Pope
    Women Who Live in Coffee Shops and Other Stories / by Stella Pope Duarte.
        p. cm.
    ISBN 978-155885-600-4 (alk. paper)
    1. City and town life—Fiction. 2. Hispanic Americans—Fiction. 3. Phoenix (Ariz.)—Fiction. I. Title.
PS3554.U236W66 2010
813'.54—dc22
                                                                2010000598
                                                                CIP

♾ The paper used in this publication meets the requirements of the American National Standard for Information Sciences—Permanence of Paper for Printed Library Materials, ANSI Z39.48-1984.

10 11 12 13 14 15 16   9 8 7 6 5 4 3 2 1

Contents

Dedicated to the invisible
city dwellers of the world.
Someday, we will all be invisible.

First, a toast to all those whose lives inspired these stories, giants of their own times, Goliaths, who have now vanished from the streets of Phoenix. They lived like shadows, like clouds of vapor in the air, yet their palpitating hearts still tell stories amidst the city's bustle and grime.

My gratitude embraces Juan Bruce-Novoa, Director of the Chichano/Latino Literary Prize, his gracious assistant, Evelyn Flores, and Sheila Ortiz-Taylor, the contest judge in 2008. Your warm-hearted welcome at the University of California, Irvine was most appreciated, and the prestigious award I received will remain one of my prized possessions.

Nicolás Kanellos, Director of Arte Público Press, and my esteemed editor, Gabriela Baeza Ventura *mil gracias* for your confidence in my work and your pledge to publish books that search the hearts of the great and small, the simple and proud, and the loved and unloved among us. Wisdom and love abound when the stories of every nation and culture are allowed to take their place in the universal chorus of storytellers.

Benny

Women who walk the streets at night are only looking for trouble. Big trouble. Mom drummed that into my head as a kid, but she never told me what kind of trouble they'd get into, so I ended up guessing. Living off Van Buren Street gave me a pretty good idea.

The street was flanked on both sides by mismatched buildings, one-of-a-kind structures that defied building codes. One old warehouse looked like a wrecking ball had struck in the center of the building and had bent the frame without breaking the windows. Some storefronts had been painted so many times, cans of paint were permanently strewn in the back alley with rock-hardened brushes, waiting for the next owner who might dream up an entirely new color.

Lots secured by chainlink fences boasted ceramic figures of conquistadores, parrots, eagles and mermaids next to black velvet paintings of Mexican heroes and mythical landscapes that leaned up against makeshift wooden stands. My favorite painting was one of an Aztec warrior holding a beautiful woman in his arms. The woman looked like she had just died. Her bountiful breasts almost brushed against the warrior's face. Adorned in feathers and a golden breast shield, the warrior appeared to be walking up a mountain into the mouth of a flaming volcano. I always wondered if he would throw the woman in or if he would jump in with her. Romantic as I was, I suspected they would both burn to a crisp.

I asked my mother about the picture, and she told me the lovers' names were Ixta and Popo. They were famous in Mexico for the great love they heaped on another. The ancient Aztec legend recorded that enemies of the lovers sent word to Ixta that Popo had died in battle. Ixta died shortly afterward of a broken heart. When Popo returned to discover that his beautiful Ixta had died, he took her body to the top of a great pyramid that later became a huge volcano. He then lay down beside her, creating another volcano, an eternal flame in her honor. To this day, the volcanoes can be seen side by side not far from the heart of Mexico City. I asked my mother if she believed the story and she said, "It's just a fairy tale. No man can love like that."

A dirt lot in between the buildings on Van Buren Street was transformed into Lencho's Tire Shop and decorated with rows of old tires dangling out from a garage front. Inside, the frame building was crammed with shiny rims, hubcaps and car stereos that were safely locked up behind wrought-iron doors whenever Lencho's closed for the day. Dudes who looked like they had been let out of a gangster movie ogled the shiny rims from the street, tracing the metal circles with their eyes, mentally sticking them on their thread-bares. Sometimes two or three would walk into Lencho's and caress the rims, brown fingers smoothing over the ups and downs of designs worked into fancy moon shapes with silver metal strips sticking out from the middle like so many moonbeams.

The more modern looking buildings were Circle K's, liquor stores and dance halls. El Paraíso was the biggest dance hall on Van Buren and looked like a Spanish *castillo*. I'd look at the top of the building and wonder where I'd seen the blocks stacked up shorter and taller all the way around until my memory produced pictures of a *National Geographic* video about Spain that I'd seen at school. El Paraíso came alive as evening drew close, especially on weekends. As the daytime sky dimmed and streetlights began to twinkle, Van Buren Street sweated and swayed with bodies, cars and music.

Mom and I rounded the corner of Van Buren and 7th on our way home from the grocery store late one summer evening as the sun was setting behind a jagged outline of buildings in the distance. I could make out the names of two of the buildings: Sunbeam Bread Company and Shamrock. It was almost 8 o'clock, but there was still light in the sky—not unusual in Arizona where the desert sets its own timetable in the summertime.

At the corner, I spotted Valentine leaning on the passenger side of a late model Cadillac. I saw her bottom first in tight stretch pants and the rest of her as we edged past the car. She had poked her head into the open car window and was talking to a man.

"Don't look that way," my mom said.

"You mean at Valentine getting into that man's car?" I asked. Valentine was one of the girls who decorated Van Buren Street like ornaments dangling precariously on a Christmas tree. She reminded me of a used-up Barbie doll, her body perfect but her face old. She was called Valentine because of the three valentines she had tattooed on her body, one on each wrist and another one somewhere under her skimpy clothes.

"Turn your face!" my mom yelled. "How we'll ever live in a place like this is beyond me." Then she started talking in Spanish. This always frightened me because I knew she only did it when she was really mad. It meant I would get it when we got home or that I would hear another two-hour lecture on the vileness of life and how girls who don't pay attention to their mothers will end up in a hellhole of trouble. I looked for gum under my shoes when my mother yelled at me. It was fun to pick at something while I was being picked on.

Actually, living off Van Buren Street in sleazy apartments connected me with down-and-outers who didn't look anymore dangerous than the cops who kept them in line. I was more scared of the cops because I had no one to protect me from them.

"Let's go back to Nana's," I told my mother.

"Never!" she yelled. "Never to that house."

"Why?"

"You don't want to know."

But I did want to know. There were tulips at Nana's house, in the yard. They lifted their bright cups up to the sun every spring, and I collected them in bunches even though Nana told me I had stopped them from breathing. No one else had tulips, and Nana jealously protected the bulbs all through winter. Neighbors passed by and wondered how Holland had come to her backyard. All Nana ever said was that they were a present to her and that she had them blessed with holy water, which explained why the bulbs survived the cruel Arizona summers.

Mom had worked at a Circle K before we moved away. She had come back mad every day because drunks made passes at her, and one time this guy scared her half to death with a toy pistol. I thought that was why we left Nana and Tata's, but maybe there was more. Mom and I packed our belongings for two solid weeks, even though all we had were boxes of clothes, books, dishes, two lamps, a worn-out mattress, a wobbly table with two chairs and an old, sagging living room couch. Still, everything was ours and it felt good to crease over the yellowed pages of my *Green Fairy Tale Book* and know that I could sleep with it again without hearing Nana say I'd go blind reading in the dark.

When we said goodbye, Nana cried and gave me two tulips, one for me and one for my mom. Mine was red, my mom's was orange. I smoothed the delicate petals over my lips and pretended I was putting on lipstick. Tata didn't say a word when we left; he kept watching TV. I thought he'd be sad but he only blinked back at the movie he was watching and pretended he had already said goodbye. I thought I had made him mad by singing too loud when he had headaches. He never once looked at Mom and told Nana to get him a cold beer when she walked us out the door.

Tata had hugged me the day before and said, "Help your ma, María, and don't make trouble 'cause you know how she gets mad." He had shuffled away, and the last I saw of him were the two white strands of hair sticking up from the top of his nearly bald head. Tata looked innocent but I knew he could get madder than Mom.

Tata was like a father to me because I never knew my real dad. I only knew his name was Benny. I found out what his name was when I got a letter from the mailbox at Nana's addressed to Benjamin Jaramillo. It was a summons for a court hearing. I traced over his name with my finger and counted all the letters, trying to make up a face in my mind. Did he have a moustache? Curly hair? Straight? My mom grabbed the letter from my hands and ripped it open.

"Just like that bastard . . . still in trouble with the law!" Then she tore the letter into little pieces before I could tell her to save his name for me.

Once, I dreamed my dad was standing in a huge ballroom with a chandelier shining behind him. I came down an enormous spiral staircase, dressed in my new jumper with my black patent leather shoes spit shined.

He was ready to take me in his arms, but the music started, and he went off to dance with a rich lady. I didn't dream about him again until we moved to Van Buren Street. I dreamed about him there because this guy who waited for the city bus where I waited for my school bus told me his name was Benny. He was tall and skinny—not much to look at, and he blew his nose a lot. Sometimes he shivered when it wasn't even cold outside. I figured he had a perpetual cold that kept him feverish. I never knew where Benny went to when he caught the bus. I figured he had a job somewhere. He didn't stay long, whatever he did, and came right back to the apartment he shared with two other guys.

I told my mother about him, and she froze in position.

"Stay away from him. He's a drug addict. God only knows what disease he's carrying."

"He looks clean to me," I said.

"Clean? Nobody's clean around here! If I had money to get us out, I'd do it now. You bet I would!"

"Was my dad a drug addict?" I asked. I was peeling a banana, pretending it didn't matter. My mother talked more when I acted disinterested.

"Yeah, he was a star addict, all right." My mother looked past me, out the window. The drapes were open. I looked out and saw two men standing by a car. One of them was Benny. Money was exchanged, a transaction completed.

"See what I mean. These people are hopeless," she said. She pulled the frayed cord on the drapes and the images disappeared.

The dream I had about my dad on Van Buren Street, didn't match what my mother told me. In my dream, my dad was tall and muscular, and he looked clean. His hair was slicked back with no gray in it, only black. His smile was perfect. He lifted me up on his shoulders. I was so high up I touched a cloud. Then I got scared because my mother looked too far away for me to reach. I wanted her to be up on his shoulders with me, but she didn't want to. She looked mad and was hollering in Spanish. Next thing I knew my dad disappeared, and I was sitting on a merry-go-round all by myself.

It didn't take me long to figure out my dad was one of the characters who walked down Van Buren Street. I just didn't know which one until my mom started working at the Dollar Store. That was when I was taken over to Lisa's apartment because my mom said it was too dangerous for me to be alone in the evenings. Lisa's apartment, was two blocks away on Jefferson Street, next to warehouses that stretched down the length of the block all the way to 10th Avenue. Mom worked until ten. Lisa didn't work at all. She collected a welfare check and waited for her boyfriend, Oscar, day and night.

"God only knows . . . a man could come in and rape you," my mother said to me. Her hands shook when she buttoned my blouse. Unconsciously, she checked me over for bruises. My mother was thin, yet smooth and round in all the right places, and men were always whistling at her. Her steps were always short and quick, like she was trying to get somewhere fast. When she talked about rape, all the nervous energy she had came up to her chest, and she shuddered like she had just seen a dead animal on the street. Rape, to me, sounded like a man was gonna take a rake to my body and scrape all the life out of me. He would leave me like a dead leaf, waiting to be crunched underfoot.

I never told my mother what I thought about rape because she was already worried about it. She looked worried when she dropped me off at Lisa's, too, and checked to see if Lisa's boyfriend had come back. I had seen Oscar once, and he looked like a black man, except he spoke Spanish. Mom said he was Cuban, and for all she knew, he carried a knife in every pocket. "They're good at knives," she told me. "How do you think Castro's been in control all these years?"

When we got to Lisa's, her cat Tumbles came out to greet us. He was orange with brown stripes running across his back. Lisa acted like she didn't know Tumbles when the landlord came around. They charged two hundred dollars for keeping a cat and Lisa said Tumbles wasn't even worth ten dollars.

"You can take care of María, but not if Oscar comes back," Mom told Lisa. Lisa didn't seem to care if I was there or not. Mostly, I played with her daughter Elida, who was eight years old like I was. We ran out of the apartment building when Lisa wasn't looking and found an abandoned warehouse with a broken window. We set up an office in the place. I was the boss, and Elida was the secretary. Other kids came around, and we made them security people and janitors. It was fun running up and down in the deserted rooms. In the corners, we saw old clothes and pee-stained mattresses. Sometimes we saw burns on the floors and walls. Some rooms we wouldn't go into because they stank like somebody had gone to the bathroom in them. Mostly, we stayed in the room with the broken window.

Elida was the first to see him through the broken window late one afternoon. He was standing with his hands in his pockets, watching us play. He had on a brown beret, cocked to one side. He was taller than my mother, but not by much. He was wearing a long-sleeved shirt, tucked into his Levi's. He didn't move much; he just stared. I got goose bumps and wanted to leave.

"He's just a drunk. He won't do nothing," said Elida.

"Haven't you heard of rape?" I asked. "He could leave us like two dead leaves."

Santiago was with us that time, but he was only seven and not much protection.

"Let's go," he said boldly. "I ain't scared." He led the way, his skinny shoulder blades curving this way and that to match his legs crossing over the windowsill. We climbed out the window, and the man stood back. When he saw me climb out last, he put out his hand and helped me.

"What were you doing?" he asked. He smiled, and I saw he had a tooth missing on one side.

"Playing office," I said.

"Nice. We need lots more offices—offices I could even walk into." Then he laughed and tousled my hair. "You're very pretty, María."

"How'd you know my name?" I asked.

"Lisa told me."

"Do you know her boyfriend Oscar?" I asked.

"Yes, I know Oscar."

"My mom doesn't like Oscar."

"Your mom doesn't like anybody," he said. By this time, he was walking by my side. I noticed his tennis shoes were missing their shoelaces. The holes with the missing laces formed uneven trails of Os over the top of each foot.

"You know my mom?"

"I heard about her," he said, "from Lisa."

Elida and Santiago were ahead of us, already crossing the street to the apartments. They signaled me to hurry. The man got on one knee to meet me face to face. He smelled like the inside of a dirty glass. His eyes were gray and looked like they had just woken up from dreaming. His hands were big, his fingers long and his nails ragged. He took hold of my hand and put it up flat against the palm of his. Our hands were the same, except my fingers were shorter and cleaner.

"Just as I thought! Another piano player," he said. "My mom gave me lessons when I was a kid. She wanted me to be somebody."

"Can you play the piano?" I asked.

"I used to, but not anymore. The music got stuck in my pinkie finger," he said, lifting up the little finger on his right hand. "The other fingers forgot how to play because the pinkie hogged up all the lessons." He laughed and tousled my hair again. "You better get home. I wouldn't want your mom to worry." He stood up and wiped his nose with the back of his hand. I saw Valentine standing at the curb, and she waved to me. The man and I both waved back.

"You know her?" I asked

"A little," he said. He repositioned his brown beret, cocking it down to a new tilt. I wanted to say goodbye but pretended I was in a real hurry and didn't have time.

I crossed the street and turned back to wave to the man, but he had already disappeared behind the row of warehouses. When we got back to the apartment, Elida started telling Lisa all about the man.

"He was looking at us through the window," she said excitedly. "He talked to María. Tell my mom what he told you." Elida was drinking a glass of Kool-Aid and got so excited telling Lisa about the man that the Kool-Aid dribbled down the side of her mouth and onto the white collar of her blouse.

Lisa had one eye on the baby in the highchair and one eye on the rice she was frying in hot oil. "You don't have to tell me if you don't want to," said Lisa, stirring the rice, and pushing a piece of cracker back into the baby's mouth. I looked at Lisa but she didn't look back. I could see the back of her ponytail swishing and her bra straps showing through her white tank top.

"I don't?"

"Not unless you want to."

I was so used to my mom screaming for answers that I blinked a bunch of times before my head cleared. It was the first time I had ever been given a choice.

"Well . . . he knew my name," I began slowly. "He said you told him about my mother. Why did you do that?"

"He asked me. He wanted to know who the pretty girl was who played with Elida, so I told him."

"He used to play the piano," I said.

"I know," she said.

"You do?"

"Oscar used to be in a band, but he never played the piano. He played the guitar."

"He said he knows Oscar."

"Yeah. They played in a band together."

"What's his name?" I asked.

"You don't want to know," she said, banging the lid down on the pan of rice.

I was ready to scream like my mother because I did want to know his name, but the phone rang and Lisa answered it. I ran outside and saw that the sun had dipped down to the other side of the world. A few kids were still playing on the street. Their bodies were silhouettes painted on orange paper. I ran past them, all the way to the stoplight, looking for Benny. I passed Santiago's apartment, heading for Van Buren.

"Who *are* you looking for?" Santigo asked.

"The man . . . Benny. He's my dad!" I was out of breath, acting crazy. Santiago thought I said "penny."

"A penny's your dad?"

"Benny!" I yelled. "Don't be so dumb."

"Benny's on drugs."

"Not *that* Benny—another one."

It was useless. Santiago's mind operated on two volts. I stood at the streetlight watching people coming out of the grocery store, and I wondered if my dad had gone in to buy some groceries. Men gathered outside the liquor store. I peered closely at them, looking for the brown beret.

Valentine was standing at the corner, and she called me over. She looked pale at night, ghostly in a pair of skintight black pants and a top three sizes too small.

"What are you doing out here so late, María?" she asked.

"Remember that man with the brown beret that waved at you today?" I asked.

"Oh, yeah, I remember."

"Where is he?"

Valentine's huge, dark eyes looked intently into mine. There was something about the way she looked at me that made tears start in my eyes. She looped her arm gently over my shoulder. She smelled good, like she was wearing lots of perfumes at the same time.

"Want some gum?" She reached into her purse and took out a pack of Doublemint. I pulled out a piece. "Here, take the whole pack," she said, pressing it into my hand.

"He's my dad," I said.

She pushed the hair out of my eyes, and I saw one of her valentines—a stenciled, purple bruise on her right wrist. "Sweetheart, he's gone. He took a bus out of here." "Where?" I asked.

"I don't know. It doesn't matter. He's okay. You need to go back home now." I wanted to stay longer, but there was a guy whistling for Valentine.

"I gotta go," she said.

I walked back down the street, past Santiago's apartment.

"You better get home, María," said Santiago's mother. "Your mom will get mad." The tears in my eyes made Santiago's mother look two times her size.

"She's looking for Benny," Santiago said.

"The drug addict?"

"No, the other one."

Santiago's mother looked at me, her eyebrows arched. "Which other one?"

"The other one—the one we met today," Santiago said.

I glared at Santiago. "I'm not looking for anybody!" I yelled and ran up the street to Lisa's apartment. I caught a glimpse of Tumbles in the hedges. His eyes were tiny mirrors reflecting back the last bit of sunlight. I let him run in ahead of me.

I thought my dad must have gone over to the Dollar Store, because my mom came home at nine instead of ten, screaming in Spanish that nobody was ever gonna kick her ass around again and make her eat dirt. She grabbed me by both arms, holding me up to her face. "What did he tell you?" she yelled.

"Who?"

"Don't act innocent, María, or I'll take my shoe off right now, and we'll settle things. Playing in empty buildings. What did I tell you?" She shook me hard.

"Leave her alone!" said Lisa.

"You stay out of this. What do you know about anything? All you do is wait for Oscar day and night."

Lisa didn't back off this time. "You can't hide her father from her all her life. It was bound to happen. You can't control the world."

"Let me handle this!" My mom shook me again and hit me over the head with the back of her hand. I was expecting worse. There were tears in her eyes.

She held onto my hand and dragged me out to the car. I thought I was gonna hear about bad girls who don't respect their mothers and end up having babies in alleys, but my mom didn't say a thing to me all the way home. She looked like she was seeing right through me when she told me to take a shower and get ready for bed. I stood under the water and let it wash away my tears. The soap got in my eyes and made it worse. By the time I got out, my eyes were red like my mom's.

Just when I was falling asleep, dreaming that a brown beret had landed on my lap, my mom walked in. She sat next to me. I didn't trust her, so I moved over, just in case she went crazy again.

"Princess," she said. I hadn't heard that in a long time. "Princess, I know you want to see your dad, but I don't think it's right. He's not the kind of person a little girl should know."

"'Cause he's a drug addict?"

"He wasn't always that way. He was handsome and funny and smart. I loved him very much."

"Do you still love him?"

"Yes . . . " My mother said the word like somebody had sat on her stomach and pressed all the air out of her. She didn't want to, but the word got out anyway.

"He told me he used to play the piano," I said. I put my head on my mother's lap.

"He did," she said, stroking my hair, "beautifully. When I heard him play, I thought I was in heaven." Her voice trembled like it was gonna die out any minute.

"Mom, why didn't he become a piano player?"

"It's a long story, Princess. Your grandma died, and they sold the piano. Your grandpa hated music. He said music was for women and sissies. But your dad had learned enough. He could play better than Liberace. And just think . . . all these years, my own father's been mad at me for marrying him. He always said musicians are liars."

"Do you believe that?"

"No. I believe your dad loves me but he can't find his way home."

"Maybe we should tell him the story of Ixta and Popo."

"Look at you! A romantic like your father!" She tickled the tender spot on my neck, and I squealed with laughter. "Maybe he *is* Popo, and maybe I'm Ixta. Poof! We'll both go up in flames and get famous!" She hugged me close, and I felt her tears on my face and hair.

"Mom," I said seriously, "he doesn't have any shoelaces. Couldn't we buy him some?"

"I don't know where to find him, Princess. I don't know when he'll be back. It's always been that way." She bent down and gave me a kiss, and then she traced a little cross on my forehead with her finger.

"He said his pinkie finger hogged up all the piano lessons."

"His what?"

"That's why his other fingers forgot how to play. The pinkie hogged up all the lessons."

"He's just playing around," she said with a smile. "Go to sleep."

Two weeks after I saw my dad, a piano was delivered to our apartment. It was kinda beat up, but it was tuned to perfection. There was lots of excitement in the complex because nobody had ever had a piano delivered to their apartment. My mom had to take the front door off its hinges so they could get it into the living room.

"I can't believe he did this," she said. She smiled and sent me over to the neighbor's to borrow furniture polish. We sold our old couch to Santiago's mother because it wouldn't fit after the piano moved in. We had to settle for sitting on our two kitchen chairs.

My mother called Old Berta on the phone to ask her about giving me piano lessons. Old Berta lived in a dilapidated house behind a string of warehouses. She had performed in Mexico City with a famous symphony before her husband got sick and they moved to the United States. She had never played here because she didn't speak English, and everybody thought she was dumb.

I always worried about my pinkie finger and wouldn't let it hog the lessons. I made sure all the other fingers got a full workout. When I got my first blue ribbon in competition, I hung it over the piano and nailed a pair of shoelaces next to it.

Devil in the Tree

The tree was so high and he was so small that the fall broke his neck. Junior fell out of the eucalyptus tree at Harmon Park when he was six. He had been talking about seeing over the tops of things before he decided to climb the tree. The tree stood at the end of the grassy baseball field close to the sidewalk I always walked by on my way to school. Junior's dog found his body around noon on a school day. By the time I got to see Junior's body, somebody had covered it with a plaid blanket, and all I could see was Junior's head, cocked at a strange angle. He resembled a baby bird who had looked too far to the right and fallen out of its nest. My first impulse was to straighten out his head, maybe put a pillow underneath it.

Reporters from the *Phoenix Gazette* arrived. Those were the days when stories about kids who jumped out of trees mattered. A detective told the reporters they couldn't take pictures of Junior's body because it was unconstitutional. He has rights, the detective said, even if he can't speak up for himself, so they took pictures of the eucalyptus tree and of Harmon Park, zooming in on faces of grownups who were standing around shaking their heads, wondering why Junior's parents couldn't keep track of him. In the meantime, their own kids were zigzagging between moving cars to get to the ice cream truck parked on the other side of the street, piping the neighborhood favorite, "Popeye the Sailor Man."

metaphor

Junior hadn't gone to school that day like he was supposed to, but instead had climbed the eucalyptus tree to see over the tops of things and had met his death. By the time the cops got there, Junior's dad Lázaro was there, crying loudly and angrily wringing his hands. He was mad at his other son Inocente who was older than Junior by three years. He kept telling Inocente he should have watched Junior and that it was his fault Junior had climbed the eucalyptus tree and broken his neck.

The fire truck finally arrived with a ladder, even though the police had radioed that it was too late for ladders. Junior's mom, Emilia, worked at the laundry, and somebody had to go get her because the cops told us not to tell her the news over the phone. The cops thought I was Junior's sister, and I didn't tell them I wasn't. I had missed school that day because I was sick with a cold. My nose was running, and my eyes were red. The cops thought I was crying for Junior, so they put me in the police car and drove me to Junior's apartment in the projects. Nobody noticed me except Inocente, who kept coming over to tell me it wasn't his fault Junior fell out of the tree. I never said a word to anybody but went into the bathroom to get toilet paper for my nose. Everybody kept thinking I was crying for Junior, and after a while, I started believing it myself. Maybe I was. I didn't know Junior as well as I knew his brother, Inocente. Inocente, who was in my fourth-grade class at school. We had been together since first grade.

The cops put yellow plastic strips around the eucalyptus tree and told everybody the tree was off limits; in fact, all of Harmon's was off limits. The black kids got the maddest because they had a basketball tournament that night, and they had to cancel. Mr. Leroy, the huge black guy who ran Harmon's told the players to shut up and get out. How would they like it if they fell out of a tree and died and everybody went on playing like it was any other day? Besides, there was an investigation going on to see if Junior fell off the tree by himself or if there was foul play. I wanted to ask Mr. Leroy what "foul play" was, but every time I was around him, I never said anything because he was so big—maybe 300 pounds, round, hard and loud—and all I could do was stare at him. He smiled a lot and never treated me bad, but one of his huge hands covered my entire head, and it made me nervous that somebody could blot me out like that.

"Sarita, don't be crying over Junior. He's gone up to heaven. Maybe he's taking a ride on Halley's Comet." He pointed to a poster hanging on the gymnasium wall of the solar system with Halley's Comet zooming by. "That comet's got a big tail, you know. Wow! What a ride he'll have on the tail of Halley's Comet!" He smiled, showing every tooth in his mouth.

Mr. Leroy told me Halley's Comet had visited earth in 1986, and that was when I was only two years old. It would come back in 2061, he said, and by then, I would be eighty years old. He would probably be dead by then. He laughed as if it was all a big joke. Twenty years seemed old to me, and thinking about being eighty made me want to ask Mr. Leroy to stop talking about Halley's Comet.

Mr. Leroy looked closely at me. "Feel better?" he asked. I wanted to tell him I wasn't crying for Junior, but I didn't want to disappoint him, so I only nodded and reached for the Kleenex he handed me.

After two days, my cold got better, and everybody thought I felt better about Junior. My mom and dad bought me a box of ice cream cones dipped in chocolate to keep me from thinking about Junior. I wanted to tell them I wasn't really thinking about him, but I didn't want them to stop buying me ice cream cones.

It wasn't until I had to pass by the eucalyptus tree by myself on my way to school that I found out things weren't the same. The hair on my arms stood up like electricity had struck me, and I stared at the tree out of the corner of my eye as I walked by. Its branches waved at me, shaking and swaying maybe trying to catch me so I could join Junior flying on the tail of Halley's Comet. In my mind's eye, I saw Junior on the fiery tail of Halley's Comet, one hand waving in the air, as if he was riding a bucking bronco.

By the time I got to school, I was sweating and panting and my eyes were huge with fear. Everybody said I was still suffering over Junior, and my teacher sent me to the nurse. The nurse looked me over and asked me if I was having nightmares. I told her I didn't remember my dreams, so she lay me down on a little bed with a white sheet over it and told me to nap for a while because I was exhausted and probably wasn't sleeping much at night since Junior died.

Later, I heard the nurse call for Inocente, and he came by because he was complaining about a headache. The nurse gave him two aspirins. Inocente had dark circles under his eyes and looked like he needed sleep. I wanted to get up from the little bed and let him sleep on it, but the nurse told him to sit on one of the chairs and wait for his father. Inocente looked at me from afar, as if he was miles away instead of in the next room. I could see him through the open door. I waved at him, and he lifted one hand up, then let it fall. I raised up on one elbow and stared at him. I wanted to tell him he didn't kill Junior.

Junior was a hardheaded brat who wanted to do things his way. Nobody could ever make Junior do anything he didn't want to do. One day he took my jacks because I told him not to. He lost two jacks and didn't care about it. I wanted to tell Inocente all this, but I didn't know how to do it without feeling guilty for thinking those thoughts about a dead boy.

10 yr old

My grades went from good to bad the year Junior died. A big worry was going on in my head, and it had nothing to do with being sad over Junior. I was afraid of the eucalyptus tree and had to discover new ways to get to school and not pass by it. There were rules at school, like being tardy to class meant you had to stay in at lunch. I was tardy lots of times because I went around an entire city block to avoid passing the eucalyptus tree with its shaky branches laughing and wanting to grab me. I wanted to tell my mom and dad about the tree, but they were already worried about me, thinking I had suffered a huge trauma over Junior's death.

Inocente left school as winter settled in and an icy haze formed in the sky, blotting out the stars at night. Trees lost their leaves and stood bare, exposing gnarled limbs, showing places where kids like Junior could climb and fall off if nobody watched them. The eucalyptus tree lost some of its leaves and kept others. Its trunk was cracked in places where insects burrowed and locusts shed their transparent skins. The white chalk line drawn by police officers from the base of the trunk to one of its highest limbs was now gone.

Everybody was saying Inocente had left school to attend classes at the psycho ward for children at the state hospital. Kids were afraid of Inocente, as they suspected he had killed his brother. I told a few kids Inocente hadn't killed his brother, but the kids kept telling me I would never know because I wasn't there until the dog found Junior's body. I didn't blame Inocente for leaving school. Nobody wanted to play with him on the playground, and nobody wanted to climb trees with him. I went over to Inocente's but had to talk to him through his bedroom window because he wouldn't come out to play or talk. He kept saying he had killed his brother by not watching him. It got so bad I decided to talk to his mother about it.

I waited for Emilia to come home from the laundry one day. I saw her get out of her friend Lala's car, her arms around a paper sack with groceries. I was standing on the porch as she came up to the door. She smiled at me, weary, her face sad even with the smile.

"Junior fell out of the tree by himself," I told her. "He wanted to see over the tops of things. That's why he climbed. Inocente didn't have anything to do with it."

Emilia stared at me as if I had spoken to her in Chinese.

"¿Cómo? ¿Qué dices, Sarita?"

I had forgotten Emilia didn't speak English, and my Spanish was rough. "Inocente, he no kill Junior!"

This sent Emilia into a wail. She rushed into the house screaming and dropped the bag of groceries. Tomatoes, bread, milk and a package of tortillas spilled out. I stood outside wondering what would happen next. Her husband, Lázaro, drove up in his truck from work and heard his wife's screams. He ran in, almost knocking me over.

"What is it? I swear I'll beat Inocente to death if he's tried to kill himself!"

He was yelling at the top of his lungs. He was afraid his wife had found Inocente dead in the house. When he found out Inocente was still alive, he beat him with a belt for worrying him and causing his wife to nearly die from fright. I picked up the groceries and brought them inside. Emilia and Lázaro were holding onto each other, while

Inocente was crying on the sofa rubbing the sores on his legs where the belt had struck.

I walked over to Inocente, and his father yelled at me, "Leave him alone! He can't be your friend!"

I was ready to ask why when Emilia grabbed me in a big hug and started crying all over me, holding me so tight I couldn't move. She kept telling me not to cry anymore over Junior. I wanted to tell her I was crying for Inocente, but she kept telling me what a good son Junior had been and how Inocente was making her life miserable—Inocente was jealous of his brother, hated him, wouldn't play with him and made Junior climb the eucalyptus tree. I kept shaking my head that it wasn't true, and Emilia thought I was shaking my head because I felt sorry for every word she was saying.

Lázaro called my father and told him to come by and pick me up because I was over at his apartment crying for Junior. He sent Inocente to his room, and I didn't see him after that. My father picked me up and told me he never wanted me to visit Inocente again. He might make me climb trees, and maybe I would fall. Then he would have to press charges with the police and have him locked up. Maybe Inocente had a devil in him, my father said, and he should have a long talk with Father Ríos at St. Anthony's Church about him.

"Inocente is innocent," I told my father. It was the first time I had realized Inocente's name meant "innocent" in Spanish.

My dad and I were driving into the setting sun. Both of us were facing bright sunlight. My dad's hat fit over his eyebrows, and he squinted and pulled down the car sun visor against the bright rays. The sun was a huge spotlight, blocking everything from view. My dad turned a corner, and the car crept closer to Harmon Park. We passed Harmon's grassy baseball field. The eucalyptus tree, its sinister branches lit up by the setting sun, waved us on. I shuddered.

"Maybe there's a devil in the tree," I said.

"The tree is only a tree. What are you saying? Who made Junior climb the tree? That's the question."

"The devil in the tree."

"There is no devil in the tree. Devils live in people."

I felt dizzy as I got out of the car. Looking into the orange globe of the setting sun had made me see spots. Mom was outside watering her plants. My little brother, Omar, was playing with dirt, digging holes and filling up a pail. Mom threw down the water hose and ran over to me, as if I had just come back from the dead.

"You never go back to see Inocente! He can't be trusted! Who made Junior climb the tree, huh? Who?"

"The devil in the tree," I said.

Mom was sweating. She smelled like earth from her plants, moisture from watering. I wanted to make myself small and grow out of one of her ribs, like one of the plants she watered, beautiful and green, forgetting all about Inocente's problems. I wanted to climb trees to see over the tops of things and never fall down like Junior did. I would prove Lázaro and Emilia wrong—all of them were wrong. Inocente didn't kill Junior! I would leave signs up on trees: INOCENTE IS INNOCENT! JUNIOR WAS A BRAT!

I pushed Mom away, angry at her for not listening to me. She dropped the water hose, and Dad grabbed it as it hissed on the ground, a knot in the plastic choking the water back. Water sprayed over his shoes and over Mom's dress.

"Sarita, get back here!" he yelled at me. "See what Inocente is making you do? Now you won't listen to us, and who knows what will happen next. I tell you, that boy has a curse on him, *un daño* that makes him bring bad luck wherever he goes."

I ran into my room and lay on my bed, crying into my pillow, crushing my big Raggedy Ann doll up to my chest, pretending she was Inocente, and I was telling him "Don't cry, Inocente, I know the truth. Everybody else is a liar." I could hear Mom and Dad's footsteps in the hall. Several times they passed my door, stopping to listen. They were afraid of me when I was mad. They wanted to keep me happy, to cure everything with ice cream cones or buy me a new pair of shoes so I would forget what I was mad about.

The sun went down, and oppressing darkness filled my room. Mom crept in, her steps halting before she reached me. She sat on the side of the bed, and I knew she was staring at me, figuring what to say. "Maybe Inocente didn't kill Junior. We don't know."

"I know he didn't. He's not a murderer. We should bring him to live with us!"

I was desperate and felt myself confusing my mother, making her doubt what she believed. I held onto her in the dark and cried into her chest, feeling the soft, fleshy body underneath her dress. I made my voice sound desperate, pleading for Inocente's life. Drama attracted my parents' attention. The more I dramatized, the more they felt they had to do something before I got sick, choked on my tongue, or strained my neck muscles. Mom turned on the light, and suddenly I wasn't acting. Light from the nearby lamp invaded the room, making everything look harsh —the pink bed cover, the lavender rocking chair, the mahogany dresser shiny with brushes, combs and mirrors set up in a row. It was too much reality for me. I wanted the dark where I could hide from a world that beat up on Inocente. Mom put her hands on my Raggedy Ann, and it was wet with tears. Her eyes looked into mine, and I knew I had won her over.

INOCENTE CAME OVER to our house on a Sunday night. Mom talked to Emilia and told her I was sad over Junior and asked if Inocente could come over for a few days and keep me company. Emilia didn't want to give her permission, but Lázaro, who was tired of seeing Inocente's pale face and dark-circled eyes, told Mom she could take him for a visit. Lázaro said God knew he had done his best by his son, but still Inocente was hard and had no conscience over the death of his brother. Dad didn't want to have anything to do with Inocente, but he relented as well because Mom kept telling him Inocente would be good for me because I wanted to help him.

Inocente slept in the spare room at the back of the house. Mom was afraid to let him hang around my little brother, Omar. She thought he might make Omar climb a tree, and the result would be the same as what happened to Junior. At night, I heard Inocente moving around, as if he was walking in circles. Once, I heard him scream, and I ran down the hall, storming into his room, my heart pounding hard under my nightgown. The back room had no window, and it was pitch-black in the room except for dim light from the hall. I could make out Inocente's body standing on a chair in the closet with a belt wrapped around his neck. He had tried to hang himself by strapping the belt over the aluminum pole that ran from one end of the closet to the other and kicking the chair from under him. Inocente's legs had gotten tangled on the chair's back, and he couldn't hang himself nor could he reach up and undo the belt. I turned on the light, grabbed another chair, set it up next to Inocente and untied the belt, my hands shaking, my fingers cold. All the while, Inocente was begging me to kill him.

"Shut up! Shut up!" I kept telling him, whispering through clenched teeth. "You'll wake up Mom and Dad. If they see you, they'll take you home, and then what?"

Inocente was coughing, gagging from the tight belt around his throat. He fell from the chair to the floor and sat there dazed, holding onto his throat.

"You don't want to kill yourself, Inocente! Stop thinking about Junior. You know he climbed the tree by himself."

"No—No! I dared him to do it. I told him he could see the world from the top of the tree. I told him if he didn't get to the top, he wasn't my brother."

I stared at Inocente, looked hard at his pale face and dark-circled eyes. "You didn't know what he would do. You didn't know he would fall off."

I held Inocente in my arms like he was my Raggedy Ann and crushed him up to my chest. The words didn't seem to matter to Inocente. It was as if he hadn't heard them at all.

"He's out there—Junior is. Mr. Leroy told me over at Harmon's. He's up in the sky flying around on Halley's Comet, and you know Junior would like that!"

Next thing I knew, Inocente was up and running out the back door. I could see his skinny white back in the dark, darting this way and that. His bones stuck out like chicken wings. He was wearing a pair of boxer shorts and was searching in the dark for a tree to climb. I tried to hold him back, but he wriggled out of my hands like a wild animal. I jumped at him, and we both fell to the ground. I sat on his stomach and held his skinny arms over his head.

"I will kill you if you don't shut up!"

By this time, I was in a frenzy, thinking of the cops coming over and spreading their huge spotlights all over the yard, and Mom and Dad screaming at me—telling me what a mistake I had made by wanting Inocente to come to our house.

"I'm your only friend!" I yelled. "You're not gonna make me look bad!"

Inocente had never seen anger like mine, and it scared him. He got quiet and finally said, "Get off my stomach. I can't breathe."

"Not until you stop your shit! I mean it! I'm tired of worrying about you and your stupid brother. Junior's gonna end up killing you!"

Inocente covered his face with one hand and cried. I made him get up and brushed off grass and dirt from his back and legs, picking off leaves with my fingers that had stuck to his sweaty skin. We walked back to his room and sat in the dark. Inocente turned on a small radio, and a waltz started to play. It was old-fashioned music, and I felt like Inocente and I were two old, retired people who had lived a hundred years. Death and murder were part of our lives, and we couldn't explain it away.

"There's a devil in the tree. That's what killed Junior," I said.

Inocente laughed like I had told him a joke. "Yeah, a devil with horns and a pitchfork. He made Junior jump." We both knew it was a lie.

INOCENTE LEFT for the Marines at eighteen. By that time, he had quit school and gotten a GED. I saw him at the Ramada Inn where he worked as a busboy. He wore a uniform for the job, and that's what got him interested in wearing a uniform for the Marines. Emilia never had any more children, and some say it was because the trauma of losing Junior closed her womb. Lázaro finally left Emilia for a woman who could give him more kids. He married one of Lala's sisters, and they had five kids. It seemed like he had forgotten all about Junior and Inocente, and if it wasn't for a few times I saw him driving down the street in his pickup truck, I would have sworn he had died.

The eucalyptus tree no longer made me shudder. I could look at it and recall, vaguely, seeing Junior dead on the ground. Sometimes I forgot altogether, and the next time I remembered, a small shock registered in my body.

Inocente and I met at the Ramada Inn before he left for basic training. He called me one summer night and asked me to stop by. He said he had a room reserved for us. I wanted to say no, but I said yes. I lied to Mom and Dad and told them I was staying overnight at Connie's, a friend of mine. I made everything sound so casual. Mom and Dad were still into drama, so I had to be careful they didn't see I was nervous about seeing Inocente at the Ramada Inn alone.

I drove my own car, a Volkswagen, to the Ramada Inn over on First Street, not far from the center of town. Inocente told me to get there by 9:00 P.M., and to come in through the back door. He had everything ready, and no one would know. I had Mom's overnight case—a small brown, vinyl bag—packed with my nightgown, a toothbrush, my makeup kit, an extra pair of panties, shorts and a blouse.

Inocente was standing by the door leaning up against the glass when I drove up. He was wearing his hotel uniform. He was tall now, much taller than me, slender and muscular from the training he had already been doing with the Marines. Suddenly, I shuddered as if I had seen the eucalyptus tree. My arms prickled with goose bumps. I wanted everything to be casual. After all, we had known each other all our lives. Inocente walked briskly out to meet me and took the overnight case from my hands. He kissed me on the lips, and it felt strange and sensual all at once.

We took the elevator to the fourth floor to a room that had been canceled out by a guest at the last minute. Lamps were on. The room was comfortable, the king-sized bed imposing. Inocente turned on the TV, and I took off my shoes pretending to flick through the channels, looking for something to watch. Inocente walked up to me as I stared at the set and put his arms around me, cradling my back up to his chest and crossing his arms around my breasts. I couldn't see his face, but I knew he was crying. Instantly, I was shaking inside. There was fear in me I had never known. It wasn't the eucalyptus tree I had been afraid of all these years.

"Relax, Sarita, relax. You never believed I didn't kill Junior, so why did you act like you did?"

"Of course I believed it." He turned me around to face him, and I saw anger in his eyes.

"I wanted you to believe me so much. You, of all people! You're afraid of me even now."

I pushed him away. "I am not! It's not everyday I go to a motel room with a guy."

He looked away from me. "I still want to die! Most days, I think I want to die. I hope there's a war somewhere and I get killed."

"Don't be stupid! That won't make Junior come back."

"I should have been buried under that tree. 'Here lies Inocente, who murdered Junior! The end of both of them!' Now I'll be able to kill, and it will all be legal."

I stared at him.

"Beat me up, why don't you?" he asked.

"You're too big. I can't pin you down like I did that day in the back yard. Besides, you don't need anybody to beat you up. You do a good job all by yourself."

We looked at each other. There was nothing to laugh about but we laughed anyway, hard, and it felt good. I sensed we were two old, retired people again. We had known each other forever. Junior's death had made us old. It loomed over us, trapped us and held us underground. We came up for air—sometimes. For minutes at a time, Junior was still alive. We were alive, and nothing had ever happened. Inocente, the Marine, took off his hotel uniform, and I stripped my clothes off before he was finished. It all seemed right. I was seeing Inocente for the first time, fear dissolving.

Nothing felt better to us than touching bare skin under white sheets. There was nothing more luxurious than lying back in each other's arms with Junior safe in the eucalyptus tree, seeing over the tops of things, maybe even rounding the corner of the universe on Halley's Comet. We'd see him again in 2061, and, by then, the eucalyptus tree would only be a memory.

Vicki's Thirteen

Vicki turned thirteen and started yelling at her mom. Her mom said that would have never happened in her family in the old days. Katrina told Vicki that in the old days, her mother did all the yelling and she just took it. Vicki didn't know for sure. Nana, on her mother's side, lived in a half-world at a nursing home. She lay on a hospital bed day and night, looking straight up at nothing in particular. Katrina didn't visit for months at a time. What was the use, she said, her mother didn't know she was there anyway.

"How do you know? I saw her wink once, twice when you talked to her," Vicki said.

"You did not!"

"Yes, I did. I pulled the sheet over her feet, and she winked at me. Her feet were cold, like icicles. Don't you remember?" Her mother shook her head.

The priest from St. Matthew's came to visit Nana and blessed her with holy oil, but nothing good ever came of it—no miracle. Other family members came by to see her for the first year and then quit coming. Ten years was a long time. Spring turned into summer, Christmas and Easter came and went. By her eighth birthday, Vicki didn't believe in Santa Claus anymore. One Christmas she whispered in Nana's ear that Santa Claus was a big, fat fake and she thought she saw her Nana smile. She baked sugar cookies for Nana and left them on her nightstand with a Styrofoam cup of milk. She would have done it for Santa, but she didn't believe in him anymore. The following week, one of the nurses told her Nana had eaten the cookies without any help. Vicki knew it was a lie, because the nurse never looked her in the eye. Instead, she turned away and left the room to throw away the liquid she had drained from Nana's catheter bag.

Vicki knew her mother wanted to yell at Nana, to shout and wake her up, make the ugliness go away, to have a mother again, so Vicki started doing it for her. She was amused when her mother looked at her, eyes shining like two black marbles, defying her to yell at her again. Katrina walked around like she was alive, but Vicki knew better. Her mother didn't know it, but she might as well have been lying in bed with Nana, feces, disinfectant and sheets with stains that nobody cared to wash away. Vicki wanted to yell at her, to scream that it didn't matter to her that they never touched each other. Nana never touched Katrina or Vicki, so they were even.

Katrina cried at the nursing home after her mother died. Vicki was there: her mother's tears were real. Vicki wanted to put her hand on her mother's shoulder and hug her, but she didn't. Once she had hugged her mother, and her mother's back had stiffened as she pulled away from her, acting like nothing had happened.

After Nana's death, the nurses left her body on the bed, covered by a sheet. Her eyes were closed, her eyelids purple. Katrina stroked the old woman's hair once, twice, brushed her lips on her forehead. She asked Vicki, "Do you want to say anything?"

Vicki was only three when Nana suffered the stroke that had destroyed her mind. All she knew of grandmothers was that they never moved. They were old and didn't talk. They wet their pants. She looked closely at her grandmother.

"Bye, Nana. This is me, Vicki."

Katrina cried again as she drove home from the cemetery after the burial. Vicki thought her mother was relieved because she wouldn't have to drive to the nursing home anymore. Her mother never cried again. She called the nursing home the next day and told them to give all of her mother's possessions to the Salvation Army. Vicki wanted to keep one of Nana's bathrobes, but her mother told her she didn't want to be reminded.

Anastacio called the house the next day. He thrived on tragedy and loved to spin it around like a top, unpredictable. He marveled at life and sighed a lot. "Ay, what a woman your mother was," he told Katrina. "Why, in the old days, she was like a movie queen. I confess I was in love with her. Then my cousin married her and drove her crazy with his jealousy. No wonder she had the stroke. Her mind gave up. I've heard of these cases. The mind snaps to protect the person from the grave." Vicki laughed when her mother told her what Anastacio had said.

"What protection!" she yelled.

"Don't get mouthy, little girl," her mother said, her hands at her hips. She was staring at Vicki. The pupils of her eyes were dark, open wide. Vicki put her hands on her hips, imitating her mother.

"What protection? Nana's dead!" she yelled.

AFTER NANA DIED, Katrina started going out with a man named Fabian, like the movie star in the 50s, she told

Vicki. He sure is an old Fabian, Vicki thought. His hair was gray, almost white.

Vicki noticed him but never looked him full in the face. She didn't think he was worthy of anybody looking at him. His cheeks were pressed in on each side, the bones sticking up like two small, smooth boulders, no dents. He always smiled even though his dark eyebrows frowned. Vicki hated it because he smiled even if you were telling him you were sick and about to die. Vicki tried it once. She told him she was sick with the flu. "That's nice," he said and smiled. Vicki looked behind his ears to see if there were any hearing aides. That was one of the only times she looked more closely at him, and then she noticed he looked at her in a new way, as if he had been waiting for her to look at him. Vicki turned away, knotting her long hair into a ponytail, twisting it into place with a brass barrette, all the while with Fabian watching. Suddenly, she was conscious of her exposed neck and the deep slope of her knit blouse.

When her mother walked in, Vicki yelled, "Where are you going now?" She wanted to add "with this idiot, this old jerk you call a date," but she walked out of the room instead. She heard her mother say, "She's mouthy now that she's turned thirteen."

"They're all like that," Fabian said.

Vicki watched his hand go over her mother's butt as they walked out the door.

NEW YEAR'S DAY PASSED them all by—with icy wind blowing over the city. Katrina had hot eggnog warm on the stove. She poured tequila into cups of hot eggnog for herself and Fabian. Vicki couldn't believe he was still hanging around. She thought he must be good in bed for Mom to keep him so long. Looking at his skeleton frame, she couldn't imagine him in bed. Maybe he was flexible, an acrobat. Maybe he did some Batman routine, wore a cape, got kinky. Vicki tried not to let herself think about her mother in bed with Fabian, but the thoughts took over her mind sometimes, and she made up scenes. When she was tired of one scene, she peeled it off her mind, as if she was changing wallpaper, and put up a new one. Often, late at night, when Vicki was too tired to think anymore, the scenes vanished from her mind altogether. Sleep overtook her, and darkness settled in. Unconsciously, Vicki sucked her thumb to put herself to sleep.

Her mother started gaining weight after Nana's death. She cooked for Fabian and stuffed food in her mouth as she cooked it. Then she set the plates down and ate a full-course meal. Her hair was turning gray. Then suddenly, one week after New Year's Day, she told Vicki she was pregnant with Fabian's baby. She was sick in the mornings, throwing up into the toilet. She dragged herself in her underwear from the bathroom to the bed, then back again. The whole room smelled like vomit. She couldn't go to work at her job at the real estate agency. Vicki got up in the mornings to help her. She hated it that her mother was pregnant. She cleaned up after her, helped her into bed and watched her curl up tight. She covered her with a sheet; her feet cold as icicles. She made sure the mini-blinds were shut all the way since sunlight bothered her mother's eyes.

"Was it like this with me?"

"Don't yell at me! Can't you see I'm sick?"

"Am I yelling?"

"You're always yelling at me. You think you're so big now, but you're still my little kid," her mother groaned.

Vicki didn't think she was yelling. She thought it was her mother's conscience acting up. If Nana was still alive, she would yell. Her daughter was having a baby from a man who was married—a man old enough to be her father. The screaming would go on for days.

Vicki sat by her mother's side and rubbed her back. Her mother's back was white lumpy flesh, warm in some places and sweaty in others. Vicki wanted to lay her head on her mother's back, absorb her pain into her brain and carry it around like a big headache.

She asked again, "Was it like this with me?"

"No. You were easy," her mother said. "You never gave me any trouble."

Vicki was relieved she had never given her mother any trouble—in the womb, at least. She asked her mother if she wanted anything to drink, and that made her mother get up again for another trip to the bathroom. Vicki waited for her, knowing her mother would be mad at her for saying the wrong thing.

FABIAN DIDN'T STAY most nights. He lived with Susana—his married daughter—and her kids. Susana hated Vicki's mom. Fabian couldn't talk to her about Katrina. He couldn't tell his daughter he was having another baby, and besides that, his wife lived down the street, and she would find out, maybe go to Susana's house and try to beat him up.

Vicki called Susana one afternoon after her mother told her Fabian had hung up on her when she had asked him for money to see a doctor. Susana's son Mando answered the phone. Mando was in the eighth grade at Vicki's school, but he was in the classroom for the "B" kids, slow learners who couldn't read above a fourth-grade level. He thought Vicki was calling to talk to him. He was friendly and flattered. Then he found out Vicki wanted to talk to his mother, and he felt rejected, as if she had slapped him in the face. Vicki told Susana whose baby her mother was having and that her dad was a gutless wonder who went around making babies he had no intention of supporting.

"It's none of your business, you little bitch!" yelled Susana. "Stay out of this. If I could, I'd beat the crap out of you, but you're just a kid. You're lucky you're not grown up."

"I dare you to try to beat the crap out of me!" yelled Vicki. Then Mando got on the phone and yelled that she'd get hers at school.

"I ain't afraid of no 'B' idiot." Vicki wanted to say more, but Mando hung up on her just like his grandfather had hung up on her mother.

Vicki checked up on her mom who was curled up in bed complaining of stomach pains. Nothing was right, and Vicki couldn't tell her mom she had a terrible toothache. One of her molars was black all the way to the gum. A huge cavity had formed in her tooth that Vicki stuffed with bubblegum and aspirin to try to make the pain go away. She was nervous about having to see Mando at school the next day, but she couldn't tell her mom. She was used to not telling her mom anything. It was the Nana thing all over again.

AT SCHOOL, Mando told everybody that Vicki's mom was a whore who went and made his grandfather get her pregnant. He told them she had a disease that made her open her legs whenever there was a man close by. By the time Vicki walked onto the campus, kids were staring at her, pointing their fingers. In the bathroom, a girl named Yaski asked her when her mother's baby was due.

Vicki yelled at her, "When is yours due, bitch?"

Yaski was bigger than Vicki, and she turned around and slapped Vicki's face. No adults were around, and nobody made a move to call anyone. Vicki charged at the girl and stuck her head in Yaski's chest, knocking her to the floor. A girl started pulling at Vicki's blouse to get her off Yaski, and two buttons fell off as the blouse ripped open. Yaski was hurt but already sitting up. The bell rang just as she staggered up, balling her fists.

The playground monitor, Mrs. Valencia, poked her head in and yelled for everybody to get out. The girls ran out, taking Yaski with them, while Vicki stood at the sink washing out her mouth. Her bad tooth was bleeding, and her face was bruised where Yaski had hit her. Mrs. Valencia noticed the blood and asked her if she had been in a fight.

"I know you have," she said. "Look at your blouse! It's torn. You look terrible."

Vicki could see Mrs. Valencia's reflection on the silver-plated surface that made up for the bathroom not having a mirror. Her face looked disfigured on the hazy surface, long when it should have been round, her eyes sunken and her ears two blurs on the sides of her face.

"My buttons fell off," Vicki told her. She looked at herself and noticed her bra was showing. The bra was one of two she owned. The straps were held together by safety pins. Clothes is more important than underwear, her mother always said, so the bra had to last. Mrs. Valencia put her arm around Vicki.

"You're bleeding," she said, straightening out her blouse, smoothing it around Vicki's shoulders.

"It's my tooth. It hurts."

Mrs. Valencia cupped Vicki's chin in her hands and looked into her mouth. "This is the worst cavity I've seen in my life," she said. "I'm taking you to the nurse. She'll send you to a dentist. Hasn't your mother seen how bad it is?"

Mrs. Valencia was holding Vicki's face in her hands, gently rubbing the side of her cheek that Yaski had slapped. Suddenly, Vicki started shaking, her body moving in one leap toward Mrs. Valencia. Mrs. Valencia held Vicki in her arms. She reminded Vicki of Nana. A memory surfaced in Vicki's mind. Her Nana was well, holding her in her arms, cradling her. They were alone, adrift. It must have been before Nana's stroke. It disappeared quickly from Vicki's mind, but it held her thoughts long enough for her to remember that she had been touched, loved. Vicki's tears and blood got all over Mrs. Valencia's dress, but she couldn't let her go. Now Mrs. Valencia was crying too. Seeing Vicki's tears and pain reminded her of her own tears as a kid. They walked out of the bathroom arm in arm.

BEFORE THE SCHOOL DAY WAS OVER, Fabian came to the school to pick up Mando because he said Vicki was a troublemaker like her mother and dangerous. "She's got no respect," he told the principal, Mr. Gardner. "She's mouthy. Her own mother can't stand her. Imagine what she'll do to my grandson, and he's got special problems."

The principal demanded answers to his questions and wouldn't take no for an answer. He called Vicki in to explain her threats against Mando. Vicki explained Mando was the one threatening her.

"Are you calling Mr. Cortez a liar?" He was looking over at Fabian.

Vicki had never heard his last name before. There was no reason for her to know it. He came over to her house, slept with her mother, looked her over, then left—just came and went like a ghost. His shadow, pencil-thin, crept up the walls of the hallway as he made his way to her mother's room at night. When he walked out in the morning, he turned off the hall light and left early enough to stop by his daughter's to get breakfast. It wasn't until Vicki heard the front door close behind him that she rolled over in bed with a sigh. Then she felt like something had lifted from her chest, and she could breathe again. Immediately, she fell into a sound sleep, her thumb stuck between her teeth.

Vicki was wearing a T-shirt Mrs. Valencia had chosen for her from the pile of clothes in the nurse's office. The T-shirt was two sizes too big.

"Look at her," Fabian said to Mr. Gardner. "Her mother can't even afford clothes for her, and her face is bruised. Probably been in a fight with her mom. Her mom should be reported to the police."

Vicki opened her mouth to speak, but Mr. Gardner signaled with his hand that he didn't want to hear it. "Young lady, you will apologize to Mr. Cortez for threatening his grandson. You ought to be ashamed of yourself. You know Mando's one of our special students."

"Special my ass!" Vicki yelled.

"See! That's what I mean!" said Fabian. "Her own mother can't stand her."

Mr. Gardner called his assistant principal, Ms. Knowles, and told her to take Vicki to the Day Suspension Room until she cooled off and apologized to Mr. Cortez. Ms. Knowles came in, looking haggard. Fleshy bags under her eyes were swollen to twice their size. Already she had had to deal with three fights, and now this. She glared at Vicki and said, "All right, let's go! Too bad we don't have padded cells." Her voice sounded like a man's, the voice of a detective Vicki had seen once on TV who led the murderer of his own wife to the electric chair.

One hour passed by, and finally Anastacio came to school to pick up Vicki. He told the school secretary Vicki's mother had asked him to pick her up because she wasn't feeling well. Fabian was still sitting in the office waiting for Vicki's apology when Anastacio walked in. Anastacio looked at him but didn't say a word. He looked out the windows and started whistling.

"If you have something to say, say it now," Fabian said to him.

Anastacio went on whistling. Fabian stood up, and Anastacio looked at him, smiling, still whistling, as if Fabian was the funniest thing he had ever seen. The secretary ran to get Mr. Gardner, and he walked in, businesslike, and explained to Anastacio that Vicki couldn't come back to school until she apologized to Mr. Cortez for threatening his grandson.

"You're full of shit," Anastacio told him. "It's this fool who should apologize to Vicki *and* her mother, and he knows why."

"Get off my campus!" yelled Mr. Gardner.

Vicki walked in, and Anastacio said to her. "Say goodbye, Vicki. You'll never see this mess again."

He put his hand on Vicki's shoulder as if he was her uncle. Vicki wanted to move away but didn't because Anastacio was all she had. She had hit rock bottom. Her rotten tooth was throbbing, her face was bruised and she was standing between two old men: one had loved her grandmother, and the other had slept with her mother.

Ms. Knowles walked in, ready to strong-arm Anastacio. She was big enough to do it, and she moved toward him as if she was on a mission to destroy him. Her baggy eyes looked like two punching bags, and there was a smirk on her face. Vicki was ready to take on Ms. Knowles, charge her head into her big belly, but stopped herself when Mrs. Valencia walked in with the nurse, who had an appointment for Vicki to see the dentist.

Mrs. Valencia told Mr. Gardner that there were two sides to every story, and she was prepared to tell him

Vicki's side. Mr. Gardner said he wouldn't listen to anybody's story until Vicki apologized to Mr. Cortez. He told her that he wouldn't tolerate anyone threatening a special education student at his school.

Anastacio and Vicki walked out together, and the nurse slipped Vicki a piece of paper with the name of a dentist who would fix her tooth for free. Vicki thanked her, and tears started in her eyes as she imagined the throbbing pain in her mouth all gone.

Fabian was standing with Mr. Gardner in his office as if he was the victim and Vicki was the criminal. "She's mouthy, now that she's turned thirteen," he explained to Mr. Gardner.

BY THE TIME VICKI TURNED FOURTEEN, she was helping her mom raise Venessa, Fabian's baby. Vicki fussed over Venessa day and night. The girls slept together and held onto each other all night, even though Venessa kicked Vicki during the night. Vicki took charge of her. She didn't want her to grow up without someone touching her. She wanted Venessa to be sure of herself and to not have to turn to old men for comfort. She watched her mother work every day, come home, drink her shots of tequila, pine over her rotten life and tell Vicki all this started when she turned thirteen and got mouthy. Fabian left her, she said, because he couldn't stand Vicki's mouth, and now Vicki could raise Venessa all by herself for all she cared.

Vicki still yells at her mom. It's the only way to reach her. She wonders when her mother stopped talking to Nana and how deep the pain must be.

Women Who Live in Coffee Shops

My mother is the founder of the <u>League of Women</u> <u>Who Live in Coffee</u> Shops, but she doesn't know it. There are times I'd like to tell her the steady stream of women who darken the doors of Sal's Diner have become her family. You see, Mom was an only child. Over the years, she wanted a sister so bad, that I guess God finally found a way to give her not one but many "sisters." Years later, I came along and made matters worse by being an only child too. Mom says it's okay for the women to hang out at Sal's. Where else can they go? To the Silver Slipper Bar so everybody can call them sluts and whores?

Sal's coffee shop sits between a Mobil Station and the Sun Dancer Lodge on Van Buren Street. The Sun Dancer may have been an uppity motel in the old days for all I know, but now it's only a shadow of what it used to be. On the motel walls facing the alley I've seen yellow spots in arcs that look like horseshoes. I imagine winos couldn't find a toilet to use, so they used the wall. Mom says never mind what they are. They just are, and that's disgusting enough.

Sal's Diner is tired and wrinkled, like a face that's seen too much. Tiles are missing on the floor behind the counter, and Sal says, why glue them back on? Nobody can see back there anyway. In the kitchen, huge grease spots loom overhead like angry eyes without eyebrows or eyelashes. Sal says, why paint the ceiling. None of the customers go into the kitchen anyway, and Fred, the State Health Inspector, only comes once a year and he's an old friend of Sal's. Contact paper on the kitchen cabinets has crinkled ridges in uneven, horizontal lines. Edges of the contact paper get unglued, and sometimes a frazzled end gets caught inside the cabinet door as it shuts. Sal says, why put new contact paper on the cabinets? From far away they look okay.

Even if you didn't know Sal, you'd know he owned the diner. He's huge, Italian, and everybody says he's retired from the Mafia. Mom's worked for him as long as I can remember. I have a problem believing Sal is a Mafia retiree because there are no checkered tablecloths on the tables at his diner and no Italian violinists strolling around.

I had my doubts one day, though, when a couple of fat, toothless guys came into Sal's wearing suits with vests and felt hats cocked to one side. They looked like the Godfather's brothers. Sal came out of the kitchen rubbing his hands over an apron he wore that camouflaged the rolls of fat he hid under a dingy T-shirt. I couldn't tell if he was excited or nervous to see the two old toothless guys. His eyes, which were usually hidden in his eye sockets like somebody pressed them in with their thumbs, were suddenly very noticeable—popping out, so to speak. The two old toothless guys picked a table in the center of the place with their fronts to the door and their backs to the kitchen.

"Watching their backs," Mom whispered as she passed by with the menus.

"From what?"

"You don't want to know."

I sat at a table with a huge panda Mom bought me to be my "brother." I named the panda bear Milo and Mom sat him up on a real highchair next to me. I pretended to feed Milo french fries, but really the only thing I was interested in were the guys at the table with their fronts to the door and their backs to the kitchen. Sal kept coming out of the kitchen to clap them on the back and talk to them in Italian, and all the while his hands waved in the air. I guessed he was low man on the totem pole because the old guys never waved their hands in the air, and they didn't clap Sal on the back.

I wanted to see if the two old toothless guys knew how to curl spaghetti on their forks like this Italian kid at school, but there was no spaghetti on the menu. The Italian kid's name was Demetrio. He looked Navajo, but he said his grandpa was Italian and taught him how to wrap spaghetti around a fork so he wouldn't have to slurp like the rest of us.

Brenda walked in as the two old toothless guys started ordering food. She worked at the Attorney General's office and didn't care who was in the coffee shop as she wasn't into status symbols. She was wearing a short white skirt and a white top with shiny sequins on the collar. Brenda always carried a huge purse that she said held everything she owned, which wasn't much according to her. She walked by the two old toothless guys and said, *"Ciao! Come sta?"* Their eyes opened wide and they looked at her in surprise.

"Bene, grazie e lei?" the bigger one said and laughed out loud.

"Bene," Brenda said. *"Bene grazie!"*

The other one moved both arms up and down like he was weighing something heavy between them *"Bella la signorina! Bella!"*

They were impressed with Brenda. Sal ran out of the kitchen because the two old toothless guys were making all this noise, and he joined them, talking so fast I saw specks of spit spray from his mouth.

"Bella e intelligente!" he said, pointing to Brenda. Sal was smiling from ear to ear because his coffee shop had customers who knew how to speak Italian. Brenda was in her moment of glory and walked back to the table and shook hands all around.

"Pusso presentarle la bella signorina Brenda. Il mio amico Giulio e Augustino," Sal said. The two old toothless guys hugged her, kissing her on one cheek, then on the other.

Brenda walked to the counter with an extra jiggle to her hips like she had just finished a movie scene. She sat on a stool and crossed one leg over the other, showing her thigh up to her pantyhose line. The skinnier old toothless guy couldn't take his eyes off Brenda's legs, and I guess I wouldn't have either if I were a man.

"Ordine qalche cosa!" he said over and over again to Brenda. "Order anything you want, anything! Put it on my bill."

Brenda whispered to Mom, "This ain't the Biltmore, but I'll try. *Ho fame,"* she said, rubbing her stomach like she was starving. *"Grazie tanto, grazie tanto."*

The two old toothless guys smiled and waved their hands, smiled and waved their hands. *"Prego!"* they shouted. *"Prego!"*

I noticed right away that most of the things they said, they said in pairs, repeating one word once, twice or three times.

"Mi bella cameriere! Mi bella cameriere!" the skinnier old, toothless guy said, pointing to Mom.

Mom blushed and waved back. I wondered about that—why Mom blushed. She was used to men complimenting her and treating her like she was their make-believe wife. Guys would sit around puffing on cigarettes, blowing smoke circles, talking to Mom like they were sitting around in their own kitchens. Sometimes one of them would ask if they could visit our house and Mom would say no. What do you think I am anyway? I got a daughter at home. That's okay, they said, as long as your old man's not around.

"Well I was gonna have a sub 'cause I'm broke," Brenda said to Mom, "but since the godfathers over there want to pay . . . well, I'll have the steak and mashed potatoes."

"Didn't know you spoke Italian," Mom said dryly.

"I don't. I read a crime report the other day at the office, and it was about these two Italians guys who owned a jewelry store. The report was so long, and there were so many Italian words, something had to stick. Didn't you know Italian is almost like Spanish? Listen—*Si* is the same in Spanish and in Italiano, *per favore*, sounds like *por favor*, *venga qui*, is like *venga aquí* and *quando*, is like our word *cuando*. It goes on and on. Shit, I thought I was going crazy when I started reading it, 'cause I could understand almost every word. Anyway, get this story—one Italian partner was jealous of the other because he stole his girlfriend, so he decided to show him up by cleaning out the store and changing the diamonds in earrings, necklaces and bracelets with rhinestones. It took him over two years to do this, as his partner was an expert in jewelry. His partner eventually got wind of the whole thing when a rich customer complained that one of the diamonds had fallen out of his wife's necklace, and when they looked at it, they found out it was only a piece of glass. He deserved it," Brenda said between bites of her steak, "what his partner did to him."

"What did he do to him?" Mom asked, stopping in midair with the coffeepot.

"Can't tell you, Andrea. It's confidential."

"How would you like some hot coffee down your back? Don't confidential me! You better tell me." Then they hunched over the counter and started talking in Spanish because the only one besides them who understood it was Camilo the cook, who was in the kitchen making an emergency pasta sauce for the two old toothless guys.

When Mom and Brenda talked in Spanish, their eyes looked different. The dark pupils darted from one corner of the white part to the other, like they were trying to keep up with their brainwaves. Everything they really wanted to say, they said in Spanish. Anything else was only pretense and routine stuff. After the conversation was over, Mom's hand was at her mouth, her eyes were bugged and all I could hear was her breath being sucked into her chest—Mom's sign of horror. I slipped Milo another french fry to keep myself from feeling jealous that I was not allowed to know what one Italian partner did to the other over a girlfriend.

THE WHOLE SCENE with the two old toothless guys might not have mattered to me, and I might have forgotten what one Italian partner did to the other over a girlfriend if Sal hadn't been arrested by the cops the Saturday after the two old toothless guys' visit.

It was midmorning on a Saturday in June, and I was talking to the bag lady, Margaret Queen of Scotland, who came by most Saturday mornings to get coffee and toast. Margaret told me she was named after Margaret Queen of Scotland and carried an old worn-out children's book with pictures of Scotland to prove her point. She had drawn a circle around a huge castle she said belonged to her ancestors. All I remember of the pictures is that there was green everywhere and wildflowers, the like of which I had never seen in Arizona.

That morning, Milo was sitting in his highchair next to me. Camilo was clattering dishes around in the kitchen and singing *Volver, Volver, Volver.* I smelled coffee brewing and garlic chicken baking in the oven. Mom was talking to Oralia and Susana from the Jehovah's Witness Assembly Hall. Oralia and Susana cruised the neighborhood on foot every Saturday, knocking on dilapidated motel doors and houses set behind industrial buildings and separated by empty fields and railroad tracks all along Van Buren Street and beyond. The days were long and hot, and the walk was monotonous for the two women since nobody opened their doors to them except ol' B. J., a drunk black man who loved company. He never listened to anything, as he was hard of hearing, so it didn't matter to him what Oralia and Susana said. It was all the same to him. Oralia and Susana carried hundreds of *Watchtower* pamphlets between them, stuffed into huge, green duffel bags, and every time they took one pamphlet out, they took them all out like a huge hand of playing cards. Which one do you want? they asked. The one about how the nuclear bomb will destroy everybody and only those who are clean will rise up into the air or the one about how adultery is the reason why so many marriages break up and why so many men end up in hell?

There was even one about how angels would come down to earth and separate 144,000 people from all the rest, and there were sifters in the angels' hands. They had been commanded to do this, as the holes in the sifters were only big enough to hold so many. Those heavy with sin would never make it through the holes. That image was especially frightening to me, and it was after looking at that picture every Saturday for years that I learned how to diet.

The cops rushed into Sal's that Saturday morning as if they were gonna arrest everybody in the place, including Oralia and Susana who had their hands up in the air just in case.

Oralia yelled, "We're conscientious objectors! You can't do anything to us!"

"Nobody wants to," one of the cops said.

The cops didn't ask where Sal was. They stormed into the kitchen and dragged him out like he had just shot somebody and hidden the body in the freezer. I guess this was before the Miranda Rights, because I never heard the cops say "You have the right to remain silent" and all that.

One of the cops yelled in Sal's face, "Do you know why we're arresting you? I'll bet you do, but you bunch of spaghetti benders never admit to anything!"

"Book him," the other one said.

"Book him for what?" Mom asked.

"None of your business," said the cop who had yelled at Sal.

"I think it *is* my fucking business," Mom said.

I was so shocked to hear Mom cuss that I grabbed Milo in both hands and covered his ears with all my might. The cop was so mad his face got purple. He looked at Mom like he was gonna jump over the counter and beat her up.

"Try it!" Mom yelled. "Police brutality is just your style!"

By this time, Camilo was out the back door. He was an illegal immigrant from Mexico and was scared they were gonna arrest him too. Mom was so mad she was shaking. She walked behind the officers as they pushed Sal in front of them. Sal was making funny noises, like he was sneezing and crying at the same time.

"Don't worry," Mom said. "I'll take care of everything."

"Call Doreen! Tell her what happened," he yelled. "Tell her to call Zach, my attorney. He'll get me out on bail!"

The cop snapped the handcuffs on Sal just as he finished saying the word "bail." The action was so sudden and forceful it seemed Sal would never see the light of day.

The last I saw of Sal, his dingy T-shirt had ridden up to where his ribs should have been, except I couldn't see the beginning or end of his ribs because everything was covered over by fat. I saw the profile of his belly sloping over his pants, sagging like a basketball that had never made it through the hoop.

On their way out, the cops almost fell over Margaret Queen of Scotland's shopping cart. One of the officers kicked it over, and everything Margaret Queen of Scotland owned plopped out in a heap on the sidewalk —aluminum cans, torn magazines, mismatched shoes, a broken umbrella, a tattered coat, the book of Scotland and two plastic headbands.

"No respect for royalty!" Margaret yelled at them. "Insolent as ever. If I had my guards stationed where they should be, your heads would roll, gentlemen—roll with no mercy! That I guarantee." She picked up one of the broken headbands and handed it to me. "Here, Joanna, take it. It will fit you just right."

The headband was only one-third its original length; one of its ends had snapped off almost to the center. Margaret Queen of Scotland said it would fit me because I was only nine years old and she was—well, royalty never told their age, she said, because it's against the law.

The cops ignored her. They shoved Sal into the back seat of the police car and drove off at top speed with their lights flashing.

"You'd think poor Sal is Jack the Ripper!" Margaret Queen of Scotland said. "Here he is minding his own business and being good to people like me who come to him for a free cup of coffee every now and then, and what does he get? A free ride to the county jail. I knew there'd be trouble when those two Italian guys came over to visit. I thought I saw them on TV. Wasn't Elliot Ness chasing them in an unmarked car?"

"That's TV, Margaret. This is real life."

"They'll probably put a big light over poor Sal's face and make him confess to murder! I know how they work, Joanna. One cop plays the good guy, and the other plays the bad one. Between them both, they can get Sal to confess to anything—even to stealing gold bars from Fort Knox!"

Margaret Queen of Scotland bent down to stick on a wheel that had come loose on her grocery cart after the cops kicked it over. "Destroying personal property. I should sue them!" Margaret forgot the grocery cart belonged to the A. J. Bayless down the street. The letters of the store, etched on the handle, had faded away after years of being out in sun, wind and rain.

Mom was already talking to Brenda on the phone when I walked back into Sal's. Brenda wasn't surprised Sal had been arrested. She told Mom they were rounding up everybody who had information on the jewelry store partners because the partner who got the worst end of the deal was dead. I later found out one of the old toothless guys, the skinnier one, was the partner who did his friend in. It surprised me any woman would want the old man, but

Mom said everybody looked old to me because I was only nine.

"What about his teeth?" I asked her.

"I guess they don't have very many dentists in Italy. Who knows? Maybe he wears false teeth and forgot them that day."

Brenda found out what was really going on in the case by reading confidential reports and giving Mom the information. I thought about the word "confidential" and knew it meant that something was a secret. If it was a secret, why was Brenda telling Mom? Mom said Brenda was a busybody and couldn't help telling everything she knew.

"I pay my taxes. I have the right to know anyway," Mom said. "Besides, how will we help Sal unless we know what the prosecutor is doing?"

One other thing stayed in my mind the day Sal was arrested. The garlic chicken burned in the oven. This happened because Camilo hid out all that day, worrying immigration officials would be waiting to pick him up. To this day, when I smell garlic cooking, the events of that Saturday play in my mind like a movie.

THE NEXT DAY, I walked over to the corner of Van Buren and Fifth Avenue to talk to Buzzard and buy an *Archie and Veronica* comic book. Buzzard owned a small shop that sold newspapers, comics, candy, cigarettes and porn magazines that he kept behind the cash register. Buzzard only had one arm, and he said it was due to fighting in the Korean War and playing with hand grenades. I don't think there was a single person in the whole neighborhood who knew Buzzard's real name. He looked so much like a buzzard that nothing else fit. When I walked into his shop, Buzzard was hunched over a stack of newspapers, reading the front page through a magnifying glass he held in the only hand he had left.

"Crazy Italians! What do I care if they all punch out their lights and go back to Sicily!" He made the word "Italians" sound like he was saying "Eye-talians."

"Sal's gone. He's Italian."

"Sal's an exception. He's learned how to be American. They should leave him alone. He ain't got nothin' to do with that murder. Everybody knows those people are always tying rocks around their feet and drowning themselves in the river."

"Why would they want to do that?"

"Because they like to sleep with fish, what else? Don't worry your little head over all this, Joanna. Don't even read any of this stuff. It will only make you have nightmares. Where's Milo?" he asked me.

"I left him at Sal's."

"Your ma knows how to manage that coffee shop. God knows she's worked there since she was a girl. I'd almost believe it was hers if Sal wasn't still around. Maybe they'll ship him back to Sicily and he'll leave her in charge."

"Is Sicily in Italy?"

"It's all the same to me."

"Where are you from, Buzzard?"

"Me? I'm from New York. My folks came over on the *Mayflower*."

"Did Sal's folks come over on the *Mayflower*?"

"Nah, they came over on the *Niña*, the *Pinta* and the *Santa Maria*—you know, when Columbus sailed, except they came the wrong way." I didn't have the heart to ask him how my ancestors had come.

On my way out of Buzzard's shop, I ran into Kay and her cousin Kamika. One of the girls was black and the other was Mexican but they both looked alike. They went to school at the New Way School for pregnant girls over by Central and Jackson. They were both due around the same time "but not by the same guy," Kay told me proudly. Both guys ran off with other girls as soon as they found out about the pregnancies. Kay and Kamika were thrown out into the streets by their families and ended up at the New Way School.

"It's really a prison," Kamika said to me one day at Sal's. "You don't want to end up there, Joanna. It's run by these strict old ladies that don't let you do anything. They're more like bulldogs. If my mom would let me, I'd go back home, but my stepdad hates me."

"Listen to Kamika!" Mom yelled from the other side of the coffee shop. "She's learned her lesson, haven't you, honey?"

Kamika nodded, took a sip of her Coke and shuffled her feet. If she hadn't shuffled her feet like that, I might have believed her, but when she did that, it seemed like Kamika was at a starting line and would do it all over again.

I knew Kamika's stepdad. He was a black guy who looked almost her age. Kamika's mother said he was older, but I never believed her. He looked like he should have been playing basketball for Central High. Mom and Brenda talked about Kamika's mom and how she must be "twice his age."

"What do you think about women who take in these young guys?" Mom asked Brenda. "I want a real man in my bed!"

"Don't put one in front of me, or I might just jump to it." Brenda saw Mom frown. "Just kidding, just kidding. Don't get worked up, Andrea."

A *real* man. I looked at Milo. His black and white panda bear face stared back at me. I wondered what it would be like if he was a teenage guy after me, a *real* man. The words haunted me. What was my dad then . . . a fake? I had seen him only twice, and that was by accident: once when my mom and him were arguing about something at a stoplight, and another time when he knocked on our door at Christmas and I happened to open it. He handed me a present and touched my forehead with a rough, uneven motion, like he was trying to rub face cream on my skin. Now every time I thought of him, his face blurred, and I tried on different noses, eyes and ears. Everything fit all wrong, and I would try again and again. All I knew was that his favorite color was yellow, and I only knew this because Mom found one of his shirts at the bottom of a stack of old newspapers one day and told me she hated yellow because it was my dad's favorite color. She took the shirt and used it as a rag to clean the furniture.

When Sal went up to testify in the case now called the "Sicilian Diamond Heist," the coffee shop was full of Mom's "sisters" the whole day long. They were on a crusade for Sal. The court system was a farce they said, judges were on the payoff. God, how did all this happen to poor Sal anyway? He only helped by giving out cups of coffee to down-and-outers and toast when they were hungry? The only man in the world who didn't make passes at them or try to grab their butts, and now he was gone. What was wrong with the world anyway? Poor Sal. How could he live in there with no real food? He'll starve. You know how bad it is when you make a fat person stop eating—they get anemic. Their blood turns pink, and the end comes quickly. Mom had the coffeepots going, and Camilo kept the sugar bowls filled. They were powerful —the women that day—all of them worried about the same thing at the same time.

"Where will we go if Sal doesn't make it back?" Susana asked Mom.

"Don't worry. He'll make it back. We'll make sure of that." Mom said this passionately, as if she had the key to Sal's cell in her hand. I looked closely at her and noticed a worry line creasing across her forehead.

Buzzard's sister Peggy came by to help with the customers. She had a bad hip with a rod stuck in it. She moved slowly, but she was the only one Mom could find to help her. I went to work too, setting tables and giving menus to customers as they walked in. Mom went down to the courtroom with Brenda to hear the case the day Sal took the stand. Peggy said she'd stay with me at the coffee shop because her emotions got the best of her, and she might end up wringing somebody's neck.

The coffee shop filled up with women the whole day. They were making plans to march in front of the courthouse if Sal was found guilty. Officers came by with warrants to check for evidence. They went through an old desk Sal had in a storage room out back. They looked through cash register receipts and files they said belonged to the federal government. Their faces were somber. They stared at the women sideways, "Morning ladies, morning ladies." One officer asked, "So, are you Sal's harem?"

Kamika's mom asked him, "You want a piece of the action? On second thought, you're kinda old for me. I like the younger set." The officer banged the door on his way out.

"Can't stand to know there's a man who just lets women be who they are. Hard ass. He should learn something," she said.

Whatever they were looking for was bad news for Sal. I didn't know until later that Mom had already cleaned out files that looked suspicious and had stored some of Sal's papers at our apartment.

There were debates all around town as to whether Sal was guilty or not. The women banded together for him. They were enraged at the system. They said it was corrupt, that everybody was on the payoff and using taxpayers' money besides. The newspapers carried stories about what they called "the women who live at Sal's coffee shop." There was talk of getting an investigation going to find out if the women were on the Mafia payoff. This further enraged women's groups in the area and made the women twice as powerful. They remembered, they said, the early days—the suffrage movement, for instance—and the struggles women had to go through just to vote in America. It took one week for Sal to finish his testimony and three months for him to be released.

The day of his release there was a knock at our apartment door. It was early, maybe five A.M. Sal was standing out in the morning light looking like a famine victim. "Lost twenty pounds" were the first words that came out of his mouth. Mom hugged him letting tears fall all over his shirt. "You saved my life, Andrea. All your women friends wrote so many letters they drove the newspapers crazy. Judges got pissed and finally decided I had nothing to do with it. I've been telling them that all this time!" Sal swung me around in his skinny arms. "It's over, Joanna." I picked up the scent of sourdough on his clothes. I noticed his T-shirt was clean and fit neatly over his belly.

"Is your blood still red?" Sal started laughing at my question and gave me a kiss on the cheek.

Mom handed him the box of papers she saved for him, and he told her thanks a million, Andrea, I owe you. Later that day, he made Mom his business partner and gave an all-day party for the women who lived at his coffee shop.

Homage

There was a time last year when I stared at my check-book and noticed I was overdrawn by eighty dollars. Imagine, overdrawn by eighty dollars after all the penny pinching I do! I wondered how much the penalties would be. The struggle for money took up a good part of my thinking and caused most of my headaches.

Walking to work every morning only served to remind me of my impoverished condition. Rushing between parked cars at the State Capitol building, I made my way to my job, filing manuscripts that detailed the crimes of society's rejects in the basement of the Attorney General's office.

Most mornings, I saw at least two Mercedes, one Lexus and what looked like a Porsche, which might have been another foreign car, for all I knew. There was a part of me that wanted to run my fingernail file across the shiny, slick surface of the yellow Mercedes parked at the entrance to the building. I looked around the parking lot to assure myself no one was around, and I actually reached for my nail file, only to stop my hand in midair. They've got insurance, I thought. A few scratches won't matter. My damage would be minimal and, at most, they'd upgrade their car's security system. As it is, cars talk if you dare touch them. Their horns blare and whine like ambulances. They threaten would-be criminals with statements like "Stand ten paces away from the vehicle," and they record theft attempts in microscopic cameras loaded in their taillights. All this while they sit motionless between painted lines in the parking lot. The twenty-first century is truly amazing!

"The rich get richer," said Amy as we both reached for the same chocolate donut at break time.

"Who bought the donuts?" I asked.

"Who knows? Probably some fat cat with money to spare."

I thought of the Hostess cupcake I had paid seventy-nine cents for at the Circle K. "Highway robbery the way prices are hiked up these days." I said. "What are these people thinking? Have they no mercy on the downtrodden?"

"Downtrodden?" asked Amy, gulping down her Pepsi. "Where did you get that word?"

"I looked it up in a the-sau-rus," I said, pronouncing the word carefully. I knew Amy had flunked reading in school. Her work at the Attorney General's office consisted of stuffing envelopes with summons for upcoming hearings.

"Poor devils," Amy said as we sat together at a long metal table after our break. She was looking at an especially thick mailing and weighing it up and down in her pudgy hands. "Wonder how much this will cost them?" she asked.

"More than they make," I answered. "They'll probably have to hock everything they have to pay attorney's fees and then put their kids in an orphanage. I hope they have rich relatives."

"Or a ticket out of the country," added Amy. She was obviously smarter than I thought.

Amy and I always worked surrounded by inanimate objects. Looming over us were shelves of files that reached up to the ceiling. Rows upon rows of look-alike manila folders stood side by side, some leaning right, some leaning left. Murderers, rapists, potheads, pimps, drunk drivers—a whole array of scumbags shared the shelves, each with a story to tell. Of course, no one was guilty. Everything was circumstance, a frame-up. Someone was mistaken. Somebody was scared into confessing to a lie. The Mafia had sent a dead fish to a juror, who then voted for acquittal. A hysterical bystander waved her finger in the air, and it pointed to the face of a totally innocent citizen, whose case was now three years old and still in court waiting for appeals. By the time the criminal gained due process, the victim had died of natural causes and the key witness had succumbed to Alzheimer's, making his testimony invalid in a court of law.

The Great American Dream was something I put in my back pocket every time I looked up at the stacks of papers waiting for Amy and me to file. Almost every page was stamped "CONFIDENTIAL." I ran my fingers over the word as I read detailed information of crimes that beat the best action on TV. "Suspect was apprehended on Fifth and Central and proceeded to climb a light pole to make his escape." Now, how smart was that? "Suspect stated she did not know the gun was loaded when she fired a full round of shots at the victim." I found out by reading into the case that the "victim," was none other than her ex-husband who had fifty counts of domestic violence filed on him. When I saw pictures of his bloodied body, I felt little compassion. I figured he had it coming.

"Amy, ever think that we're getting immune to right and wrong?" I asked.

"Immune?"

"You know, like we don't give a shit one way or another."

"We don't have much choice working in a place like this," she responded.

Another point for Amy, I thought. I looked carefully at her and wondered if she had been zapped by electricity from a cracked cord the night before. Her hair still looked straight, so whatever had zapped her had caused minimal damage.

"I had my eyebrows done," she said, taking off her thick glasses to show me the curving arches of her eyebrows minus stray hairs. Eyebrows were Amy's thing and she had them professionally taped and trimmed twice a month. It was a pity I couldn't see her brows behind her glasses. The lenses acted like a reverse pyramid, causing her eyes to look shrunken. I felt as if I was looking from the base of a pyramid to its point, far away in the distance.

"Nice job." I said. To myself, I asked the question: Why would a woman who is 150 pounds overweight bother to have her eyebrows done? One more conjecture: Who cares? We worked as slaves for a buzzing, corporate mongrel of deadbeat clients and wiser-than-thou preppy-babes who walked through the jungle of paper wads and unreturned phone messages like a herd of elephants eating their way across the landscape. The deadbeats felt dwarfed by the pompous splendor of diamond rings, Rolex watches, duplicates of degrees *summa cum laude* hanging on the walls and, exacting, manicured nails.

Now, there was something I could identify with: fingernails. Fingernails intrigued me. Amy had her eyebrows, and I had my fingernails. I scrounged up money every week by adding water to the dishwashing liquid so I wouldn't have to buy a new bottle, lining the garbage can with newspapers so I wouldn't have to buy garbage bags and throwing all the clothes into the washer at the same time to avoid wasting laundry soap.

It all worked together somehow. The kids only got mad when something red turned everything pink and they had to suffer for a week with pink T-shirts while the color faded. It was worth it when I saw my french-style acrylic nails, polished to perfection, poised over the word "CONFIDENTIAL." They looked like they belonged to someone else—to one of the preppy-babes, for instance. I felt justified in doing my nails because at least I could see them. Amy had no way of looking at her eyebrows, except through the eyes of others.

Taking a deep breath before rising to start filing, I heard the swoosh of the elevator.

"Someone's coming to our dungeon," I said. Amy smiled. I liked to make her smile because the rolls of fat around her throat all moved collectively, like a kaleidoscope of human flesh.

"It's Mr. Jenkins," Amy said, importantly.

"So what?" I said.

Amy put her index finger up to her lips. "Shhh."

"Hello, ladies. Are you down there?"

His voice reached us before we saw him. "Where else would we be?" I answered.

"Brenda, quit. You'll get us in trouble," Amy said.

"My, my," said Jenkins as he walked into our cage. "I had no idea you had this much to do."

"Mr. Jenkins, if you only knew," I said. His crew cut bristled a bit as I said the words.

"Uh, Ms. Gomez, isn't it?"

"I've been called better," I said, extending my hand to shake his. I made sure my nails tapped his palm lightly. "It's my ex's name."

"You *do* speak Spanish, don't you, Ms. Gomez? he asked.

"I've got a handle on the language," I said. Amy's eyes opened wider, and I actually saw some of the smooth flesh right below her eyebrows.

"Could I impose on you a bit, Ms. Gomez?" he asked, looking a little startled. He gazed at me from between the stacks of papers piled at either end of the table.

"Name your game," I said. Amy stifled a gasp.

Jenkins looked into my eyes, then away. "Well, it's actually a matter of translating. I've got a couple of clients in my office who only speak Spanish. I wonder if you would do the honors."

"Honors?"

"Uh, I mean, would you come in and translate?"

"What happened to Mr. Ramirez?" I asked. "I thought he did all your translating.

"Actually, he was apprehended for drunk driving last night . . . and well, as you know, the laws are pretty strict about things like that."

"In other words, he's in the can?" I said.

"To put it bluntly, Ms. Gomez. Yes."

"Then I *will* do the honors," I said. "I'm good about helping my people that way."

As we walked to the elevator, I whispered to Amy, "Stop shaking, he's only probate." I winked at her and she slid her glasses back up her nose.

"Probate?" she asked. I knew the old Amy was still alive.

I felt Jenkins giving me the up-and-down when we were in the elevator. Scum, I thought. Probably uses his job to pick up women.

"I don't believe we've ever met before," he said.

"Belief, Mr. Jenkins, is more an attitude than a fact, if I may be so bold."

"Very reflective of you."

Jenkins looked at me like I had wet varnish all over my clothes. I kicked off one of my shoes as we made our way to the twelfth floor.

"I hate these shoes," I said. "I don't know why I wear heels. My feet are deformed, Mr. Jenkins. Bunions, you know. My mother never had enough money to send me to a podiatrist."

"She must have sent you somewhere. Your vocabulary's wonderful!"

"I'm a self-starter, Mr. Jenkins. I had to be. In a family of ten kids, it's dog eat dog to get to the dinner table. You move fast or you end up with crumbs or somebody's leftovers. The weak don't survive in a world like that."

"I should say not. You should be proud you made it out of there."

"Not proud, Mr. Jenkins, just appreciative that I knew when my mother served dinner." Jenkins laughed out loud, his shoulders shaking vigorously.

"You are truly refreshing, Ms. Gomez."

"In a world like this, it doesn't take much," I said. "By the way, call me Brenda if you like."

"Brenda? I like that. I'm Jasper—named after my grandfather who led a bunch of Confederate soldiers in North Carolina."

We walked leisurely into Jenkins' office, which was plastered wall to wall with photos of him playing golf, skiing, riding a horse and standing next to a clown in a scene that looked like it had been clipped right out of The Wizard of Oz. The office was permeated with the smell of hardwood mixed with the dank odor of overstuffed furniture. I knew Jenkins had brought in his own decor to impress the seamy side of society. Amy and I had to sit on state-issued furniture in the basement, and it wasn't nearly as glamorous or comfortable.

In one of the plush, leather chairs sat a middle-aged woman. Her graying hair was swept back into a bun, and enormous gold loops hung at her ears. She was neatly dressed in a black pantsuit and a pair of sandals. Opposite her sat a man with brown, curly hair, a western shirt, Levi's and boots. All that's missing is the cowboy hat, I thought, then noticed the hat tucked under the chair. A Mexican Texan. He gave me the up-and-down like Jenkins.

Jenkins introduced us all around. I shook hands with Señora Rivas and her brother Efraín Gutiérrez.

"Sit here, Ms. Gomez," said Jenkins, leading me to a straight-backed chair. My rotten luck. The only time I had gone into one of the attorney's offices and I had to sit on a chair that had no give. I arranged my hands on my plaid skirt and noticed how the lavender polish contrasted boldly with the greens and browns of the fabric.

"Now, where shall we begin?" asked Jenkins.

"The beginning would be a good start," I said.

Jenkins leaned back in his chair, smiling broadly. "Okay, this is the deal. Their mother owned the property currently in probate, which sits in what is called *Las Cooatro Milpas*."

"*Las Cuatro Milpas*," I corrected. "The Four Cornfields."

"Anyway, their parents bought the land in or around 1930. Their father died several years ago, the mother died last year. There is no Will to designate a legal owner, and there are three thousand dollars of back taxes owing on the property."

I translated the grim facts to Señora Rivas. She gasped in surprise. She glared at her brother, asking him what had happened to the money she had sent him to pay the taxes. His eyes shifted nervously, and he reached for his hat under the chair. He held it in his lap, fingering the rim. Her voice raised several pitches before he looked at her and simply told her he had needed it. War would have broken out, except Jenkins was there to quell the impending disaster. If I had had it my way, I would have voted for letting Señora Rivas go for her brother's throat.

"Ask them about a Will," he said.

"*¿Un testamento?* Is there a Testament?" I asked.

At this, Señora Rivas produced a crinkled piece of paper folded into several squares. She handed it to me, and I noticed it was the remains of an ancient paper bag. I held up the parchment to the light and finally made out the faint outline of words written in an elegant scrawl. The message designated Anna María Gutiérrez as the legal owner of the property. She pointed to herself as the same person named in the document.

"I can't accept this," said Jenkins in frustration. "What kind of a fool do they take me for?"

"It's signed by her mother," I said.

"How do you know?"

"*¿Ésta es la firma de su mamá?*" I asked Señora Rivas. She attested that it was, and she pointed out the signature of the local priest who had witnessed the event.

"A priest signed as a witness," I said. "What more do you need? Would a priest lie?"

"I'm not in a position to prove things true or false at this point, Ms. Gomez. I'm simply trying to get at the facts. I don't think this paper will be admissible in court."

"Why?" I asked angrily. "Because it's not written on a computer? They were poor. That's all they had to write on. It's a legal document."

"Nobody'll buy that," Jenkins said. "Besides, they owe back taxes, and I doubt they can come up with the amount."

"Are you telling me they're gonna lose their property over three thousand dollars?" I sensed my heart beginning to thump. "You haven't even asked them if they can come up with the money."

"Obviously, they can't," he said flatly.

"How dare you make assumptions you can't prove!" I accused loudly. "What's so precious about a measly piece of land in a barrio, anyway? There's gotta be a gimmick."

"The State wants the land to build the new baseball stadium," Jenkins said. "Their property will be condemned and turned over to state officials."

"I knew it!" I said. "I knew this was bourgeois stuff!" Tension in the room was high. By this time, I had forgotten all about my nails and was ready to crack the phone receiver over Jenkins's head, thus ending my days as a translator. "There are loopholes for *everything*," I said, punctuating the last word. "Loopholes as big as hula hoops! You know it as well as I do."

Jenkins looked solemnly at the document before him as if he were studying an Egyptian scroll. After squinting and frowning for a few seconds, his eyes lit up like he had just discovered the tomb of King Tut's twin brother. "You know, Ms. Gomez, because you're so gutsy, I'm gonna help them," he said brightly.

"Don't pay homage to my guts, Mr. Jenkins."

"There is absolutely no understanding you, Ms. Gomez!" Jenkins said in exasperation. "What is it you want?"

"Why don't you try paying homage to honesty, integrity and sleeping at night with a clear conscience?" I said. "You know . . . the traditional things."

"Are you telling me I've bought into the system?"

"Get a clue, Mr. Jenkins. You're on the other side of the desk. I'm not. The Confederacy's not around anymore."

He leaned forward ready to pounce, then suddenly changed his mind. "I wasn't part of the Confederacy. My grandfather was. I haven't bought into this whole thing, I can guarantee you that!"

"Prove it," I challenged.

"Tell them I'll help them."

I related the news to Señora Rivas and her sidekick. They were elated. Señora Rivas got up from her chair and swung around the desk to hug Jenkins and kiss the top of his crew cut. Her brother shook his hand and blew me a kiss.

"See! Without your act of benevolence, you would have missed this display of gratitude," I said.

"*Dile que no le va poder,*" said Señora Rivas.

"The lady says you won't regret this," I translated. "That means get ready for tamales every Friday. You *do* like tamales, don't you?"

"I've lived in the Southwest all my life. Of course I do."

"Then you've got it made in the shade," I said.

Jenkins smiled again and stood up as happy as Señora Rivas and her brother.

"Doing anything after work, Brenda?" he asked as his clients walked out of the office.

I knew he was scum when I first laid eyes on him. Picks up women every chance he gets. Wait till I tell Amy.

"Not much, Jasper," I said. "What about yourself?"

The Plight of Patrick Polanski

Myron told me Patrick Polanski was a big-time boxer back east. He almost fought Joe Louis but lost his bus ticket and never made it to New York. I didn't believe Myron because he lied about everything. He was always in trouble at school, giving Mr. Sanders, our eighth-grade teacher, a run for his money. It wasn't until I visited Myron in prison fifteen years later that I got to know the real truth about why he did the things he did.

I was more like Myron than I wanted to admit. Neither of us was the apple of anybody's eye. I learned those words from a song at church. His dad beat him up most every day, which was why he ran over to Patrick Polanski's place. Me? I just sneaked over there because there were too many kids in the house, and my ol' man was hopping mad most of the time. We made a real weird trio because Patrick was Polish, I was Chicana and Myron was black. This went on for three months before anybody found out. When people did find out, they said all kinds of crazy thing—like we were part of a drug ring and were victims of child pornography. I didn't know what pornography was back then but would have understood if somebody tried to act nasty with me.

I stopped by for Myron at his house on school mornings and we'd walk the five blocks to Edison Junior High, taking shortcuts through the Central Projects and the local park where city workers spent hours in their company trucks eating lunch and wondering when the layoffs would start.

When I'd walk into their house, Myron's mom was usually at the ironing board steam ironing their second-hand clothes. "And proud of it," she would say, pointing to the clothes on the ironing board. "Proud my family's starched up and don't have to wear no flour sacks for clothes like I used to—and that's the truth!"

She got to talking about Patrick Polanski one morning a couple of weeks after he had moved in two blocks down the street. Adults were curious about a white man moving into their neighborhood, and their suspicions were like sparks flying: darting glances were hot embers, and small explosions turned into muttered curses against a white man who dared to take up residence in their own back yard. We kids were curious, but in a different way. None of us had ever been close to a white man before except for our teachers at school.

"Patrick's a no-good drifter!" yelled Myron's mom from her position at the ironing board. "Prob'ly done some time back east. Prob'ly a thug back in Chicago, a mobster."

"No, he wasn't," I said.

"Now, how y'all know that?" she asked. Her hands were on her huge hips, and all of a sudden, I lost all my strength from the middle on up.

"Just guessing," I said.

"Well, y'all guessed wrong! And you best be staying away 'cause those kind don't know what to do wif it half the time."

"Do with what?" I asked.

"Never you mind, Ceci. I know your mama don't want you to go near no drifter like Patrick." She grabbed Simie, Myron's seven-year-old sister, as she walked slowly by and jabbed her in the back.

"Get ready for school, fool! Yo' hair ain't even combed!"

"Let's go, Ceci," Myron said. His eyes said, 'Let's go now!'

"See you, Mrs. Kingston," I said. "I'll be sure Myron brings his books home so he can do his homework."

"God knows, that boy don't do a lick of homework. 'Sides that, he's a liar. Wif books or wifout, he lies."

"I'll tell you if he has homework," I assured her.

We got out just in time. Myron's dad was hobbling into the dark living room. His right shoe was torn all the way across the toes, and a dirty sock stuck out. I looked for blood on the sock but saw none.

"I got a injury," he said, pointing to his foot. "Bad injury. I been outta work 'cause of it." Myron's dad had the ragged curtains of every window closed tight. Looking out the windows at the world wasn't his idea of a good time. "Ain't nobody look'n in, and ain't nobody look'n out," he said. He lived by the code of darkness. The darker the room, the less he could see the squalor around him. I always thought he looked like a dark stone sitting in a cotton field.

The sagging couch boasted cushions split in two like pictures of cotton plants I had seen. The stained carpet was worn to a frazzle and smelled like yesterday's dirty diapers. Bugs ran rampant everywhere. The Kingston's didn't keep them as pets but they came pretty close. They left crumbs on the floor for the cockroaches to nibble at so they wouldn't get into their shoes. The darkness in the house added to the mystery of what was under your feet as you walked in.

I watched Myron next to me as we made our way down the street and was amazed at how clean his shirt looked. Besides the ironing, I knew his mother washed their clothes with Ajax when she ran out of laundry soap. Her own huge, mismatched clothes didn't matter to her as long as her kids had clean, unwrinkled clothes. Myron's shoes were tattered, but his jeans looked new.

"Salvation Army," he said, pointing to his jeans. "They delivered clothes to the needy at our church last Sunday."

"Nice," I said. I looked at my own clothes bought at the secondhand store—Goodwill stuff. My mom had spent hours at the store trying to match pants to blouses, skirts to jackets.

"We buy at the Goodwill," I said. "Sometimes at Woolworth."

"Your ol' man working yet?"

"He got laid off again. It's been raining too hard for him to go back."

"Still fighting with your mom?"

"Every day."

"So's mine."

Myron and I had been friends since kindergarten. We made it official one day after Mrs. Powell, our kindergarten teacher, sentenced Myron to a corner of the classroom. He stood there crying big, watery tears that made his nose run and got his hands full of snot. Besides all that, he had peed in his pants. Mrs. Powell was so mad she wouldn't even give Myron a Kleenex so he could wipe his nose. When she wasn't looking, I ran and grabbed a Kleenex from her desk, then sneaked over and gave it to Myron. He just looked at me, his dark eyes reaching for mine over the edge of the dirty Kleenex. It was then I knew I'd never leave his side. He was cornered, helpless and waiting for his mother to pick him up to change his pants and beat the crap out of him.

Maybe that's why I made friends with Patrick Polanski. He was cornered too. His face looked tired, as if his features were fading away. By the time I saw him, he had all but run out of eyebrows. They were only faint outlines over each blue eye. His forehead was long with a few wrinkles. He bore a red scar on his left cheek, close to his ear. He said his mother had done that to him before he was taken away from her and put into an orphanage. "I think she was trying to iron out my ears," he said laughing. I wanted to show him the stripe on my back my dad made with his belt buckle, then decided not to.

The back of Patrick's head was balding slightly. The rest of his hair was bushy and gray, creased in some spots, puffed up in others. He wasn't very tall—not much taller than Myron. He wore a perpetual outfit of secondhand brown khakis, a wrinkled shirt and work boots. His khakis were faded at the knees. Whoever had worn them must have worked all day on his knees. Maybe they were faded because Patrick prayed before the image of a black Mary hanging on his wall. "The Black Madonna," he said. "Isn't she beautiful?" Patrick told us the original painting of the Black Madonna had been damaged in a church fire in Poland. Someone restored the painting, but left the Blessed Mother's skin black and that's how she acquired the name, Black Madonna. Myron felt right at home staring at the Black Madonna. Rosaries dangled on either side of her picture and a wooden crucifix hung in the space next to her. "I got that from a monk in Pennsylvania," said Patrick, pointing to the crucifix. "It's got a real splinter from the cross of Christ." I went up to the crucifix, noticing details, wondering where the splinter was located.

"That's the only family I've ever known," Patrick said. "Just those two." He made the sign of the cross over himself reverently.

There was a look of innocence about Patrick—a clear-eyed anticipation, like he was still at the orphanage waiting to be adopted. I could see how someone could have mistaken him for a kid long after he got to be grown up. The nails on his right hand were yellow, he said, from smoking cigarettes and from catching yellow fever from a Chinaman.

"A real Chinaman?" I asked.

"Yeah, the cook at the orphanage," he said. "He was always putting his yellow fingers into our food."

"Did that make the food taste different?"

"Sure did! Tasted like yellow squash."

"Is that the truth?" asked Myron who liked to gather stories to add to his lies. We were sitting at Patrick's kitchen table, which was nothing more than orange crates stacked up on one side of the wall. Patrick opened up the checkerboard and brought us a fresh bowl of popcorn.

"As far as I remember, it's the truth."

"In Chicago?"

"No. I never lived in Chicago. I lived in New Jersey."

"Why'd you come all the way to Arizona?" asked Myron.

"I got tired of all the stuffy people back east."

"That's a long trip," I said.

"I've been moving all my life," said Patrick. He coughed and sniffed a bit.

"Going from place to place and going nowhere."

"Where do you want to get to?" asked Myron.

"Somewhere where people are friendly, where I don't have to be afraid."

"Afraid of what?"

"Of the things people say, of the things they do. Lots of folks don't want somebody like me living too close to them."

"Why?"

"They say I'm a drifter 'cause I ain't got no family. I never got along with too many people except kids. I never had none of my own."

"I'd let you live at my house," said Myron, "but you wouldn't like it. My dad's real mean, and my mom yells a lot."

"I'm used to living alone. I had a few friends but they're dead by now. Most of them are people others call tramps—you know, people that live on the streets."

"Were they in the orphanage with you?" I asked.

"Yeah, one of them was. The place was filled with nuns, Catholic nuns with big, pointed hats. They screamed at us and burned our hands if we didn't behave. Sometimes they put on Halloween masks and jumped at us from the dark to scare us." Patrick looked at me, his eyes misty. "Why did they do that to us, Ceci?"

"I don't know. That was mean." He put his hand over mine. I held onto it. I felt like I was his older sister and he was my little brother. I had to protect him from the scary nuns with the Halloween masks. Then Patrick gave me a wet kiss on the cheek, and I pulled away, startled by his abrupt movement and confused because I had never been kissed by a white man before.

BY THE TIME Myron and I got to school that morning, Patrick had already been picked up for questioning. Myron and I always split up when we got to the playground to avoid the hooting and hollering of the kids. They called us a variety of names: Salt and Pepper, Brown and Black and the Two Oreos.

Stella Pope Duarte

Myron had just gotten to the basketball court and was sinking a few shots into the hoop when I heard my name announced over the loudspeaker. "Cecilia De Leon, please report to the principal's office." I didn't know which was worse, the fact that I was being called to the principal's office or the fact that I had just heard the name "Cecilia" over the loudspeaker. Everybody called me Ceci. Cecilia was Dino's wife who lived down the alley from us, the one with her butt sticking up in the air like an oversized pillow. She cussed like a Marine sergeant and beat her husband up on a regular basis. "I didn't name you after her," my mother had told me. Still everyone said, "Just like Dino's wife," even though I exercised everyday to keep my butt from sticking up in the air.

I rushed into the principal's office hoping whatever it was would be quick. If it was bad news, I wanted them to give it to me right between the eyes. I hated to wait. Trapped feelings made me nervous. Hit me with the belt or throw a lamp at me, but don't just stand there looking at me. I don't like it when I don't know what's coming at me. I comforted myself with the thought that my mother probably needed me at home. One of the kids was always getting sick, and it took all day at the clinic to get help. It wasn't unusual for me to miss school so I could help my mom at the clinic.

Shannon, the principal's secretary, pointed to one of the office chairs "Wait there" she said.

I could hear the back-and-forth conversation of a two-way radio coming from Mr. Webb's office. I stood up and noticed a police car parked outside. My mind leaped into a panic as I made up flashes of news I might hear. Maybe JuJu, my little brother, had been hit by a car. Maybe my dad got into another fight with my mom and the neighbors called the cops. A sinking feeling started in the pit of my stomach, the coming down part of a Ferris wheel ride. Mrs. Salisberry, the nurse, walked in.

I stood up. "Somebody sick?"

"No, Ceci. Just relax. I want you to come with me."

"What for?"

"Just to talk." I stiffened. There was no use arguing with Mrs. Salisberry. Her words were orders, prescriptions that weren't written down. She had her stethoscope hanging around her neck. I instinctively looked for any evidence of needles. Was it shot time?

"Sit down, Ceci," she said as we walked into her two-by-four office. "Mr. Webb wants me to talk to you about a situation." She sat straight up in her swivel chair. Behind her, the eye chart swam before my eyes, and I read the fourth line in my mind with no problem.

"Ceci, do you know the white man who moved down the street from the Kingston's recently?"

"You mean Patrick Polanski?"

"Yes, Mr. Polanski."

"We call him Patrick."

"Who are 'we'?"

I felt like I had already said too much. "Whoever knows him."

"What do you know about him?"

I looked at the eye chart again. "Look at me, Ceci. Don't be nervous," she said. An old familiar feeling of being cornered came over me. What was she after?

"I only know stories. Some might be true, some might be lies."

"What kinds of stories?"

"Is Patrick in some kind of trouble?" I asked.

"Yes."

"What kind of trouble?"

"I can't tell you right now because the police are going to investigate."

"Where is he?"

"They've taken him away."

Then I started blurting out all kinds of things because I imagined Patrick Polanski in his faded khakis, cornered between two police officers, the scar just under his ear wet with sweat.

"He's Polish. Very religious. He's got a picture of the Black Madonna or something like that with rosaries hanging all around and a crucifix with a splinter from the cross of Jesus. That's his family, he says. His khakis are faded at the knees from praying so much. He's never done anything to anybody. He's my friend—mine and Myron's. He was raised by Catholic nuns in an orphanage, and they scared him into being good by wearing Halloween masks when it wasn't even Halloween. And . . . . " I felt like I was drowning, standing in a swimming pool with no bottom.

"Hold on, Ceci. Don't get upset."

"But he's my friend."

"Yours and Myron's?"

"Yes."

"Who else?"

"I don't know."

"Did Mr. Polanski ever put his hands on you?"

"His hands? He hugged me once." I thought of Patrick's kiss and blushed.

Mrs. Salisberry tilted her head, hanging on every word I said. "Hugged you?" She took out a pen and wrote down something on a piece of paper. I had never seen her look at me with so much interest.

I tried to explain. "He hugged me after I beat him at checkers." Leaving the part out about the kiss made me nervous.

"Where were you playing checkers?"

I was in too deep. My mom would find out I had been going over to Patrick's, and Myron's mom would be boiling mad because Myron was with me, so I lied. "At the park."

"Did you ever visit his house? I thought you said he had a holy picture and a crucifix."

"Well . . . yeah. All the kids go over there sometimes. He gives us popcorn and candy sometimes." This doubled her interest. She leaned over and looked intently at me. "What else do the kids do over at his house?"

Everything I said seemed to make Mrs. Salisberry think of all kinds of crazy things. Seeing myself trapped, I started to cry.

"Now, Ceci, you don't have to cry or get nervous." She handed me a Kleenex. "Do you know what the word 'molest' means?"

"Yes."

"Listen to me carefully, Ceci. Did Mr. Polanski ever molest you?"

"No! Is that what you think? He's just a lonely old man. He's never hurt anybody!" I almost shouted the words.

At that point, Mr. Sanders, my eighth-grade teacher walked in. He put his arm on my shoulder, and I went on crying. Mr. Sanders' touch comforted me, and I wanted to ask him in a whisper if Patrick had molested me by giving me a kiss.

"I think this is enough, Mrs. Salisberry. Ceci is a girl who can be trusted to tell the truth. I think she should go home if she feels this upset."

When I got back to the office, Myron was there, his eyes twice their size. He was the kindergarten kid again, standing in the corner.

"Mr. Sanders talked to me," he whispered. "What happened to Patrick?"

"I don't know, except they took him away," I whispered back.

Before long, Mrs. Kingston stormed in, crying and making a big fuss. "Didn't I tell both of y'all that drifter was nothin' but trouble? Children nowadays don't listen to nothin'! Just does all they pleases and gets their poor parents in trouble." She grabbed Myron roughly by his shirt collar. I knew she wanted to smack him, but she held her anger in because Mr. Webb and the officers were there. They had a woman with them.

"I can take Cecilia home," the woman said. "Her parents said their car isn't running."

I felt sorry for Myron as I saw him whisked away by his mother. There was no escape for him. My fingers were ice cold.

"Cecilia, I'm Mrs. Scott, and I'm here to help you."

"I don't need any help!" I said loudly.

"Ceci, we want you to go home with Mrs. Scott," said Mr. Webb. "You'll be safe with her."

Safe from what? But nobody was talking. The officers were busy writing in their notebooks and calling on their two-way radios.

"Don't worry about homework, Ceci," Mr. Sanders said. "You just take care of yourself and let Mrs. Scott take you home. Everything will be all right." He smiled gently, and his eyes looked right into the part of me that was shaking with fear. For an instant, I wanted to let Mr. Sanders put his arms around me and hold me close.

On the way home, Mrs. Scott asked me how well I knew Patrick Polanski and if I would be willing to go to court to tell the judge about him. When I asked her what

I should say, she said, "Whatever really happened and don't be afraid."

I know now that nightmares can go on during the day because they happened to Myron and me. My parents were so mad at me because I had been over at Patrick's that my dad pulled me by the hair and threw me into my room. "Don't think you'll get out of there, you little bitch!" he yelled. I figured Myron was getting worse than that —maybe even ripped open like Mr. Kingston's old shoe.

My mother cried when I had to be taken over to the doctor's office by Mrs. Scott to be checked for "possible molestation." The doctor never gave me the results but it was the worse time I ever had in my life. I closed my eyes and pretended my private parts weren't being looked at. I didn't tell the doctor about the kiss. I knew he'd tell my mother and she would say I let it happen.

Next thing I knew, our names were in the newspaper, and I started to understand what was being said. Myron's sister Simie had been molested by a man she described as none other than Patrick Polanski. I had never even seen Simie at Patrick's and wondered what the accusation was all about. I asked my mom one day after my dad had left for work.

"They found pictures of kids at Patrick's house," my mom explained.

"But he likes kids," I said.

"Too much!" she yelled. Then she went on and on about how wrong I was to hang out at Patrick's and how all the neighbors were saying I wasn't a virgin anymore and that we would all have to move away because of all I had done by hanging around with a child molester and a black kid.

"He was looking for friends," I said. "All I saw was a Black Madonna and a crucifix with a splinter from the cross of Christ."

Still, my mother raged on. We ended up moving two months later. I tried going back to school, but it was no use. Boys talked dirty to me, and all the grownups looked at me with pity.

Myron moved away before I did, and I lost track of him until fifteen years later when I saw his name at the Perryville Correctional Facility where I was hired as a parole officer. I read all his paperwork and found out he had assaulted his dad because he was trying to defend his sister Simie, and he killed him, striking a fatal blow with a crowbar. He was charged with second-degree murder and was serving a twenty-year sentence.

Myron still looked to me like the five-year-old kid in Mrs. Powell's class, except he was tall, over six feet. His long arms dangled way below his waist, and just looking at him brought tears to my eyes. "Patrick was innocent," he said, as we both talked in my office. "My ol' man confessed to the whole thing. It made me crazy because we had told the truth all along. 'Course, nobody believed me back then, all the lies I told." He reached into his shirt and pulled out a small crucifix on a silver chain. "Patrick gave me the splinter from the cross of Christ. I smashed it into this crucifix. Who knows what he really gave me, but it's worked somehow. I can tell the difference between a lie and the truth."

"I wondered what ever happened to that splinter. But then, living like you did, I can't blame you for all you did. The newspapers ran the whole story a year later. I knew it had something to do with your dad. Patrick was released to a nursing home four years after the whole thing happened."

"Life's a bitch, Ceci. My ol' man dead and my mom still saying he was innocent. Simie knows the truth."

"God does too," I said.

"That's what I'm counting on," Myron said. "How's your folks?"

"My mom finally left Dad, and as far as I know, he lives over on Filmore with a prostitute. It was hell for me, Myron, but I won't ever regret being your friend. Here . . . take this," I said, watching tears start in his eyes. He blew his nose on the Kleenex.

"Still taking care of me, huh?" We both laughed.

"I visit Patrick at the nursing home every other week. I just have to stay out of the range of those kisses. God knows that man never learned how to be affectionate without almost knocking somebody over. All that checking they did on me . . . you know they examined me, don't you?"

"Yeah, my mom told it to everybody. Sorry-ass people if you ask me."

"Well, at least I can identify with some of my clients."

"He kissed me once, you know. I can tell you I thought I had let him molest me. Shit, I was going crazy over it. Do you think he really was a pervert?"

"Maybe he was. I got no evidence on that. He was our friend, and we had never had a white guy for a friend before. He made us feel special."

"That's what perverts do, Myron, before they strike. I've heard of all kinds of cases since I've worked in parole—tragic cases, most of them. I was so desperate as a kid to be close to a man who didn't yell at me, I guess I ignored everything I felt around Patrick."

"Was he a pervert, Ceci?"

"Maybe in the past, but not with us. I think he was a lonely old man, as lonely as we were."

"As lonely as we *are,* you mean." Myron glanced at the bare walls and sighed.

"Yeah, and cornered too. I always hated that."

"And the Black Madonna? What ever happened to her?"

"What do you think, Myron? Remember, that was his family. He's probably got the picture at the nursing home."

"Now *her*, I can identify with!" Myron slipped the crucifix tenderly back into his shirt.

"Tell me the truth, Myron. Is there really a splinter of Christ's cross in that crucifix you're wearing?"

"Feels heavy to me." He stood up acting like he had a fifty-pound weight around his neck.

"You gonna be my parole officer, Ceci?"

"Nope."

"Good then yeah, it's for real."

Mismatched Julian

Mom decided Cousin Julian needed help, so we took him in. I noticed right off that his right foot didn't match his left, and one foot pointed out, and the other pointed in. His eyes weren't aligned correctly. One was low on his face with little space for an eyebrow, and the other was high with space enough for two eyebrows. One eye looked like it was staring at you straight on, and the other looked like he was looking just beyond your shoulder. I looked at his ears closely, hoping they matched; they didn't. One was flat and flared out in the right direction, and the other was more a tight circle that hadn't flattened at all. My mom said not to stare, but the more I tried not to stare, the more I stared. It was winter, and Julian had on thick pants and two sweaters. I couldn't see his arms, elbows, knees and legs. When Julian walked, his steps took him first to the right, then to the left, until you'd think he'd turn around and face you with his back. He shook my hand, and I noticed there were ridges on every knuckle. Mom said it was arthritis and told me I had to shake his hand very carefully to avoid giving him more pain. I was afraid of the fleshy knobs, the arthritis and the pain. When he shook my hand, I didn't let my hand make a circle over his. He smiled, and I noticed his lips were the only thing in his whole face that matched.

Mom made Julian comfortable in the only armchair we owned—a swivel that lived a double life. It could swivel toward the living room and face our tiny thirteen-inch TV sitting on a bookcase. It could swivel toward the kitchen table so a person could eat comfortably by bending toward the table, grabbing the plate and adjusting it on his lap. Utensils, cups and glasses could be left on the table within reach.

"Looks nice, Sabrina," Julian said to me one day as he nibbled on Fritos.

"What does?" I asked, not knowing what he was staring at as he sat on the swivel, facing the kitchen.

"Your place. That little candle over there." He pointed to a candle in a small glass container that Mom kept on the kitchen windowsill, to keep the place looking warm in the mornings, she said. Mom liked cozy places, and according to her, the candle at the windowsill made our apartment look cozy to people on the outside. It didn't matter to me what people on the outside thought. Our apartment was one of the crowded apartments in the Duppa Villa Projects, and "cozy" was not the word I would use to describe it.

Frankly, I didn't think it mattered to Henry P., the weasel-like man who lived in the apartment to our left. I asked the old weasel one day why he added the letter "P" to his name, and he said it was force of habit. There were two Henrys at the manufacturing plant where he had worked all his life, cutting sheet metal and welding. His boss had added the "P" so he could figure out which Henry he was talking to.

Henry P. sat every day on a broken kitchen chair on his front porch. In between drags on his cigarette, he coughed and pounded on his chest for oxygen. Sometimes he coughed so hard and got so much phlegm out of his lungs that I was afraid his next breath would never come. Before Henry P.'s wife died, she had decorated their porch with huge plants in ceramic pots. She said she had heard they give off oxygen and that would help Henry P. breathe. In my mind, the plants were absolutely worthless for Henry P.'s breathing: in fact, they made the air dustier and harbored small swarms of gnats that lived in the leaves of the larger plants.

Our neighbors to the right weren't people I wanted to impress either. They were a retired couple who planned their lives around the television shows they watched all day long. There was a daily lineup of TV shows: *Good Morning, Arizona; All My Children; General Hospital; Let s Make a Deal; The Andy Griffin Show* and so on. I knew them by heart because I could hear them through the wall of my bedroom, which faced their living room. Esther and her husband Marvin were a mixed couple. Esther was Mexican, and Marvin was black. They told me that in the old days, everybody kicked them out of wherever they went, and at last, because of Dr. Martin Luther King, Jr. and other leaders, they were allowed to live in peace.

Straight across from our front door lived Doña Lenny, another person I didn't care to impress. Doña Lenny walked with a cane, and her hair was entirely white, fitting over her head like a skullcap. In my mind, she had one foot in the grave, except she kept defying the odds by staying alive year after year. No one knew Doña Lenny's real name until she passed out in her apartment and knocked over one of her parakeet cages. The chirping of the birds was what drew attention. The cops went through her identification and found her name was Katherine Dubois. The name sounded French to all of us, and we were shocked to think she had lived with us in the projects posing as a Mexican.

Every room in Doña Lenny's apartment contained cages of parakeets. She treated them as a gigantic feathered family. Her children refused to visit her, and Doña Lenny said it was because they were jealous of the birds. She remembered every bird's name, from Holly to Franco, to Reyna, but she could no longer recite the names of her four children.

Eventually, Julian arranged Doña Lenny's parakeets in their cages by degree of color. For all his mismatched ways, Julian craved order and things that matched. I had never dreamed that gradation of color in parakeets could be so intriguing, but after they were arranged by yellows, greens, limes, oranges, tans, blues, whites, darker, lighter, everything made sense. The birds chirped and sang in small, sacred tones that meant something to other parakeets and nothing to people. They seemed content and less fussy and spent their days preening each other. Management at the projects ended up making Doña Lenny get rid of half her parakeets because neighbors next door complained about the odor of parakeet crap. The fire marshal visited her apartment and declared that the newspaper she used to line the parakeet cages posed a fire hazard and that her apartment could not be used as an aviary.

I asked Mom several times when Cousin Julian was leaving, and every time I asked, she said she didn't know. Things weren't right for him to leave was her answer.

"What things?" But she shrugged her shoulders and turned away. This made me so mad that I looked for ways to make Julian's life miserable. In his room, I mixed up every sock in his drawer and caused havoc in his closet by mixing up the colors of his pants and shirts. Julian's urge to match things was incredibly strong, and I knew he would go through everything in his room and match things up to perfection again. He never mentioned to Mom what I had done.

Julian was the cause of new smells at our apartment. There were the sour odor of Julian's socks in the clothes hamper, a musty strawberry smell to his sweaters, the shocking sensual smell of his aftershave and, around his body, an odor of unwashed hair and baby drool.

Our refrigerator and kitchen shelves were filled with unfamiliar brands of foods. Julian loved pasta in all shapes and sizes, lentil bean soup and yogurt bars. The small trashcan in his room overflowed with potato chip wrappers, Snickers candy bar discards and shells of sunflower seeds. It seemed Julian had taken over our apartment, so I stayed in my room most of the time playing my stereo on high volume until Marvin or Esther pounded on the wall.

Not long after Julian came to visit, the candle on the windowsill that was meant to impress our neighbors threatened our lives. The glass container burst, and flames started eating away at the plastic blinds. It was Julian who stumbled into the kitchen when he smelled burnt plastic. We heard him yelling for Mom and me, and his voice sounded like it was coming from every room in the apartment. By the time we got to the kitchen, he had pulled down the blinds and thrown them into the sink. He had used dishrags to smother the fire. He had everything under control and was watching Mom and me, smiling as if he was Smokey the Bear and had put out a blazing forest fire. One of his hands revealed blisters across the knobby flesh.

"Get me some ice," Mom said to me. She could have gotten it herself, as the refrigerator was one step away, but she wanted me to do it. She looked at me like she was saying, *See, your cousin can do something right.* I looked back at her, *He was just lucky.* Mom put the ice cubes in a plastic sandwich bag and pressed the bag over Julian's blistered knuckles.

After that, Julian took credit for saving our lives and felt important. Henry P., Esther, Marvin and Doña Lenny came by the next day. Julian told the story over and over again until it wasn't just the kitchen blinds that had caught fire. The fire had roared from room to room, and he had saved us in the knick of time, just before the fire hit the water heater and blew up the place.

I had my doubts. For one thing, Julian had been fascinated by the candle flame, and maybe he had been looking at it more closely and had caused it to fall and set the blinds on fire. I told Mom, "To save our lives, he might kill us."

"Don't be ridiculous, Sabrina. You're exaggerating. He's a perfectly peaceful man. His family never wanted him around, so he doesn't know how to live in a house."

I found out Cousin Julian's family was from Napa Valley in California. They grew grapes for wine but weren't very successful at it. Their grapes had to be mixed in with big ranch owners' grapes, and the money earned was barely enough to pay the mortgage and keep the vineyards in seed. In fact, it had been rumored that the reason Julian had come out mismatched was because of poisons used as pesticides on the vines. Another rumor my mother clung to was that Julian's mother, her aunt Hilda, had been an alcoholic all her life, living off the juice of the vines. This destroyed Julian as he formed in her womb, and the result was the man who now shared our tiny apartment in the projects.

Julian didn't have any wrinkles, so I couldn't tell how old he was. My mom figured he was twenty-seven. She came up with the figure by counting through the ages of Aunt Hilda's five other kids. I asked Julian if he had ever been to school, and he told me his education consisted of going to the same class for twelve years at a school for kids who were special. "You know, different—big heads, no lips, no legs, respirators and kids who played with balls of string all day."

"What did you do all day?" I asked him.

"I helped the kids with the big heads put their hats on. I helped kids with no lips sip milkshakes through straws. I adjusted the oxygen for kids on respirators. I pushed the kids with no legs on their wheelchairs and made big balls of yarn for kids who played with the string."

Looking very serious, he leaned closer to me. "There's a secret there," he said.

"Oh, yeah? What is it?"

"The kids never really grow up. They live in Never-Never Land, and they don't even know it. You know, with Peter Pan and Tinkerbell. You can count on them to give you love. Without them, the world would be lopsided—not enough love."

He laughed, slapping his thigh with the palm of his hand. I laughed, too, at the strangeness of it all and wondered how Julian had helped all those kids with his mismatched body.

Mom said Julian was disabled. A check came for him every first of the month. On days the check was scheduled to arrive, he sat on the couch since it was closest to the front door and the mailbox on the porch. When he heard the mailman open the lid of the mailbox, he jumped to his feet. If the first day of the month came on a Sunday, Julian felt happier, as that meant his check would come in one day early, on the last day of the month. After I found out about the disability check, I thought I had an answer for Julian's visit: his check. That turned out to be a lie. It took no more than three days for Julian to spend all his money. He loved buying gags and small gifts for the neighborhood kids at Ali Baba's Magic Shop close to the apartment. He sometimes spent money on look-alike potholders and dishtowels, matching sheets and pillowcases, sets of cheap necklaces and earrings for Mom and me and scented candles he set up in his room. I didn't know it then, but Julian was also lending money to people in the projects and sending some home to his mother.

Lyndon—this kid at school who liked me—came by one day. He was a champion wrestler, and I had made the Mat Maid cheer line, which kept us close together during tournaments. I found out after practicing with Lyndon that I could be pinned down in twenty-five different ways. Lyndon's body was stocky, his muscles taunt. His thighs felt rock-like when I ran my hands over his legs, pretending I was only learning another wrestling move. He wasn't handsome with his brown hair sticking up in back and his long, white face, but he made up for it with his body. He didn't look much like a ninth grader. Lyndon looked more like a high school senior. His hands felt like warm bands around my arms and back when he touched me, bands I wanted to stay wrapped in a little longer, but then the move was over. I noticed his body was bruised and scraped, like he had been in a traffic accident or fallen off a roof. He said that's what athletes had to look forward to—wrecked bodies.

Julian walked in. He took a look at us and got fascinated by wrestling, as he had only seen it on TV with big dudes from the world championship leagues. Lyndon showed Julian a few moves, and it looked so funny to see Julian's awkward body twisted and turned every which way. He was so out of balance he fell down a few times, laughed, got up and fell again. His athletic ability had never been challenged, so he had no limits. Julian tried to match weakness to strength. Every time he got pinned, he stayed still and said "Uncle! Okay, I give up!" I kept telling him he didn't have to say that, but he forgot. There was sweat on Julian's forehead forming tiny beads that trickled down to his eyebrows, but he wouldn't quit. Mom walked in and told us to stop tormenting him.

Julian only laughed. "I've been tormented before. This is nothing."

On Saturdays, I went over to Lyndon's to visit. His family had moved to Arizona from Texas. They looked like hillbillies to me, but I think I was wrong about that because hillbillies don't come from Texas, or at least that's what I've been told. Lyndon's family lived in a huge, ancient house that looked like a storm could blow it away. In fact, years after they left, a storm did blow most of it away. The house was framed wood, discolored by the weather, its roof showing bald spots where the tarpaper had come loose. It looked like somebody had painted the house red in the past, but now it looked pink. It had two floors with a real balcony extending from one end of the front to the other. Lyndon called the balcony a "veranda." I told him a veranda was a screened porch that houses in the South had, but he insisted it was a veranda. The wooden beams were permeated with termites that had eaten through the wood, leaving gaps and jagged splinters that crumbled to the ground like they had been put through a meat grinder.

Lyndon told me his uncle had fallen through the balcony "drunk as a skunk." He said "my uncle was walking on the veranda when nobody told him to, and then down he went and landed on his feet. Drunks don't get hurt. They're flexible," was his explanation.

Lyndon never asked me into his house. I saw his mom through the screen door, an immense, formless mass of flesh, sitting on the couch. Her name was Wanda. I knew that because her sister lived with them and yelled at her all the time. Lyndon's little sister, Lizzy, came to the door and poked her tongue out at me, and when Lyndon wasn't watching, I stuck my tongue out at her. Lizzy's blond hair was tangled and looked like it hadn't seen a comb since she was born. Her clothes were ragged, faded to no color in some places, and wrinkled in others. Mostly, she wore no shoes. Lyndon yelled at her, "Get in, you little tramp!" I didn't like it that he called her "little tramp," but didn't say anything to him. I knew she should be in school, third grade maybe, but she missed school every other day. Truant officers from the school came over to Lyndon's house, but the family had excuses, illnesses and problems, so they went away.

I let Julian come with me to one of the wrestling matches at school and from then on, he came to all the matches, even practices and preliminaries. He sat on our side and cheered for the team—even when every guy had been pinned down and we were down to zero points.

Coach Andre took a liking to Julian and made him a water boy of sorts. Julian took the job seriously, arranging paper cups in rows of four around a big orange water cooler. He made sure there were clean towels for players exactly where they left their jackets and backpacks. He cheered in twos, "Way to go! Way to go! . . .Go Champs! Go Champs!"

The noise of the crowd yelling with angry voices disturbed Julian. He pulled the cap Coach Andre had given him over his eyes and ears. I didn't know if he was hiding his mismatched face or trying to keep the sounds out.

Once, this man—a skinny, scrawny guy with a pointed head—from one of the other teams threatened Coach Andre. He said they had called a penalty on his son, and what the hell was wrong with them? Were they blind? He asked Coach if he had learned his stuff in a back alley. He went on and on, even after security threatened to escort him out the door.

Julian came between the guy and Coach Andre and asked him if he wanted a glass of water. I was watching and knew the guy was ready to punch Julian out. I waved my hands from the Mat Maid cheer line, hoping Julian would see me and understand he had to get out from between them. In one quick motion, Julian grabbed one of the cups filled with water and threw it in the man's face. The guy was so surprised he didn't do anything for a few seconds. He just stood there, gasping. My hands went over my mouth and the crowd roared all at once. I thought the next move would be the scrawny guy's fist in Julian's mouth. What really happened was the guy's son came over to jump Julian, and just then, Lyndon ran up and knocked the guy to the floor. Coach and the scrawny guy rushed over to stop the fight. That was the day Lyndon got kicked off the team for the rest of the season. Julian, head down, hands in his pockets, looked like he wanted to go through the floor.

The scrawny guy and his son got kicked out of the place, and the match went on without them. "Lyndon's gonna hate me," was all Julian muttered over and over again.

I kept telling him he wouldn't, and Lyndon kept telling him the guy and his son were crazy. This was the third time they had acted up, so who cares?

Still, nothing penetrated Julian's mind. Coach Andre called Mom to come get Julian, and she had to walk him out of the gym by the elbow. His steps took him to the right, to the left, and finally out the gym door.

IT TOOK THREE DAYS for Lyndon to convince Julian no harm had been done and the wrestling matches would continue over at his house. Lyndon set up some boards and borrowed a few mats from Coach Andre so he could construct his own wrestling ring. He set up the ring in the middle of the hard-packed dirt that made up their backyard. The property was bordered by a sagging chainlink fence and littered with old tires, a baby buggy, tools, a lawnmower that didn't run, an old wheelbarrow with rusty wheels, empty milk cartons and what looked like a storage room leaning on its side.

Twice I heard Lyndon's mother yell through the kitchen window, "Lyndon, you stop with all your mess!"

Her sister answered, "Shut up, Wanda! This whole fucking place is a mess!"

Then a squabble started between them, and I heard little kids crying. Pretty soon, Lizzy came out to ride on an old tire swing tied to a dead mulberry tree. Julian took one look at Lizzy, and his eyes teared up. He walked over to push her on the tire swing, and she giggled like any other little kid would, even though she stared hard at me when she could. I thought maybe Lizzy reminded Julian of the kids at the special school.

Within a few weeks, Julian had the whole back yard looking picture-perfect. His matching habits went into high gear as the back yard was a complete wreck, and there was enough for him to do for days on end. He was happy as he worked, whistling with Lizzy at his side, helping him. Spring days and warm afternoons with the smell of orange blossoms passed us by as the wrestling matches continued, and Julian got Lyndon's back yard matched to perfection.

Wanda called Julian into the house one day, and I'll never know for sure, but I think she wanted him to match up the whole house. Before long, Lizzy was running out of the house in perfectly matching outfits I knew Julian had bought for her. Her hair was combed neatly for the first time in her life, the blond hair shiny, sheen and smooth as gold. Her barrettes matched her socks. She still stuck her tongue out at me sometimes, but she did it with class, as if she was a princess and I was the kid who did her laundry. I told Julian to stop matching Lizzy up, because she wasn't related to us, and he said he'd stop, but by now, he was obsessed. Little by little, Lizzy took the form of a swan-like, lithe figure—a real princess out of an English fairy tale. I absolutely hated her but pretended it didn't matter. Julian is crazy. What does he know? Lyndon didn't call Lizzy, "little tramp" anymore, and every boy in the neighborhood was after her.

Julian's matching was driving me crazy. The whole house was in pairs, mirror images, look-alikes; all my underwear arranged by colors, tags down; my socks in lumpy matching bundles. I looked into Mom's eyes to see if she had had enough.

"This is why they threw him out!" I yelled at her. "Can't you see? He's a weirdo, Mom. He's got the whole neighborhood looking like a postcard!" I threatened to leave and go live with Aunt Hilda unless she did something about Julian.

Then, before I knew it, summer was over and autumn had come, leaves falling, golden, the color of Lizzy's hair, and Julian was all packed up in his room.

"Shoving on," he said. "I've done all I can here." I looked at him and by now was trained to imitate the one eyebrow up, the other down. I looked in the mirror and noticed I looked like Julian, perfectly matched. My nightgown, my slippers and everything was color-coordinated. I had given up. I didn't even know freedom was coming and wasn't sure I knew what that meant anymore.

Doña Lenny, Henry P., Esther and Marvin came by to say goodbye with donuts in matching pink boxes. Mom made coffee, and Julian set up the breakfast table with plates, cups and spoons set exactly right.

We were all staring at each other. Esther took two bites of her donut, and said, "We'll miss you, Julian."

Marvin nodded twice and said, "We'll miss you, Julian," and took two bites of his donut too.

I felt like I was in a horror flick. I broke up the match by saying, "Well, I hope you get to wherever you're going and stay there!"

Everyone glared at me, and Julian shrugged one shoulder up, one down and took two bites of his donut. Doña Lenny gave him pictures of her parakeets in cages, all color-coded. Henry P. disconnected himself from his oxygen tank and drove Julian down to the bus station.

As soon as they were gone, I shut the door and started un-matching everything, pushing chairs up against the walls, moving the couch in a diagonal position, running my hands in my chest of drawers and balling up my underwear. Mom sat on the swivel chair crying for Julian because she said he had a disease. He had to give the world what he didn't have: perfection and order. I laughed like Dracula and ran wild, throwing towels out of the linen closet and tearing clothes off hangers to mix up pants and blouses. After my rampage, I took note of all I had done, and everything was a wreck. Mom was still crying over the horrible person I had become. Now she knew why Cousin Julian left, she said.

Around midnight, I got up, and in a daze that lasted until morning, I matched everything back up again.

One of These Days
I'm Gonna Go Home

Peggy Wolf took a trip to Nogales and came back with a Mexican girl, an orphan named Emma. Peggy had heard about the orphans in Mexico from Reverend Cameron, pastor of the Church of Christ in Phoenix. Reverend Cameron told his congregation that the plight of the Mexican people was a disaster, poverty so widespread, he said, it defied the imagination. This was 1989, and nothing had changed in that country for hundreds of years. He went on to describe cardboard boxes that served as houses set up along the border between Arizona and Mexico, stuck up, he said, wherever there was space on bare dirt—some with newspapers for roofs. People begging, children and mothers sitting out on the sidewalks with their hands reaching for a handout, was what you'd see.

"What kind of a godforsaken, low-down society are we, anyway?" he asked. "If we're not part of the solution, brothers and sisters, we're part of the problem." Then he puffed up his square chest and yelled, "You're the one God needs out there!" He pointed one finger at the congregation, waving it around like a loaded gun and settling on a few faces for greater emphasis. One of those faces was Peggy Wolf's.

Peggy was crying through the whole sermon, remembering the crowded Bronx apartment she and her brother Buzzard had lived in New York when they were kids. Rats as big as squirrels rampaged around in the garbage, defiantly running through rooms and sometimes sitting up on their hind legs to take a closer look at the Wolf family. Buzzard would get his baseball bat and start chasing them, hoping to hit a few, but instead, they chased him at times—even sinking their teeth into the old, wooden bat and biting off a piece. Peggy and the six younger kids jumped up on chairs and couches. Sometimes they'd even hang out the fire escape. If their dad was home, he'd take pot shots at the rats with a cork gun he had fashioned to daze the rats. If he was lucky, he would conk the rats on the head, make them dizzy, then rush in with a nylon net, run outside to a tub on the back stoop and drown them. His wife was so used to this that she kept up her housework—ironing, cleaning, doing dishes—all the while yelling at the kids for running up on the chairs and couches. If this wasn't bad enough, there were cockroaches with wings like bats that made their way into the Wolf apartment through the sewers. As a kid, Peggy fought off the flying missiles even in her sleep. She thought maybe the kids in Mexico were putting up with rats the size of Chihuahua dogs and cockroaches larger than hamsters that stung and laid eggs big as a hen's.

Peggy told Buzzard she was gonna adopt an orphan from Mexico and that was that. There was no use trying to make her change her mind. It was made up, and her conscience was clear. God knows she'd do anything to protect someone from what she had gone through as a kid.

Buzzard told her she was crazy. "Ain't we got enough troubles already?" he asked. "We're barely gittin' outta the mess we made of the Coney Island joint that went to hell in a hand basket, and now this?"

Peggy didn't care that their Coney Island hot dog stand had gone to hell in a hand basket. Buzzard still had his magazine stand down on Van Buren Street and his pension from the Army for fighting in the Korean War, that should be enough. Peggy was convinced she had to go get an orphan from Mexico. God was telling her not to forget the lost and lonely, especially the children.

She packed an old flowered, canvas suitcase with a pair of jeans, black slacks for dress-up times, two dresses for Sunday wear, a few blouses, a couple sweaters (might get cold at night in March), sneakers and flat dress shoes besides her underwear and a few cosmetics. She didn't pack clothes for the child, as she didn't know what age the child would be, but she did bring along a stuffed giraffe, coloring books and crayons.

Peggy decided to drive up to Nogales alone because it would take a few days for all the paperwork to go through to adopt an orphan, and nobody in the congregation could afford to take off work. She was nervous because she didn't speak Spanish, and she worried that she might say something embarrassing and people would laugh. Reverend Cameron told her not to worry. "There are members of our church already there. Some of them speak both English and Spanish, and they'll help. Besides, God is watching, and He'll cover you over with protection."

THE METAL BRACE in Peggy's hip started to act up. Tension, the doctor said, and he told her to avoid long trips and stepping on the gas pedal too long.

"It's too late," Peggy told him. "I'm headed for Nogales, Mexico this weekend, and that's a four-hour drive . . . then back to Phoenix, and that's eight."

The doctor shook his head and doubled up on her arthritis medication, which didn't help the brace since it had nothing to do with arthritis. Peggy had undergone a hip replacement two years ago after cracking her hip in a bad fall at the age of twenty-five. Her cousin Uranus, schizo from the day he was born, had chased her down the hall of an apartment building on one of her visits to her mother in New York City. He wanted Peggy to get him a pack of cigarettes and when Peggy said no, he ran after her and made her fall down two flights of stairs. Since then, Peggy had worn a fake hip with a brace stuck in it. The whole thing started out being "heavy to carry," as Peggy described to the doctor, but he kept telling her it was all in her mind and that the metal brace was really only a pin. "Think of it as a knitting needle," he told her. The knitting needle image frightened Peggy, as she had been jabbed in the arm as a child with her grandmother's knitting needle. Now Peggy had to struggle not to think of the metal pin as a knitting needle. Instead, she thought of it as an aluminum rail—the kind she had seen shining on door frames in the buildings downtown. Aluminum's lightweight, so Peggy soon learned how to lift her leg off the ground with ease and only a slight limp.

Buzzard told Peggy she was crazy for everything she did, but this time he told her she was really crazy for driving to Nogales alone to adopt an orphan she knew nothing about. "Don't wanna hear nothin' about it," he said, angrily swiping at his runny nose with a stained handkerchief he grasped in his right hand. His left hand was gone just below the elbow, shot off by grenades during the Korean War. Buzzard kept the stump of his left arm hidden inside a folded up long-sleeved shirt. "Don't wanna hear such craziness. I thought I was nuts to be a goddamn grenade specialist, but this is the pits. You've gone over the edge this time, and you're not taking me with you!"

All the while, Peggy was going over the accounts, adding and subtracting figures in a tattered black book, trying to figure out how she'd get the extra money she needed to make the trip.

"That's another thing," Buzzard told her. "Your clear conscience's got a price tag!" He finished wiping his nose and sat with a thud on an armchair to watch TV. He had already read the newspaper at his magazine stand and didn't want to watch the news, so he watched cartoons. He looked over at Peggy and mumbled under his breath, "Women shouldn't be traveling alone, adopting orphans all over Mexico, for God's sake. Ain't we got enough troubles? And the kid's not even the right color. How will we talk to the orphan—supposing we do—since we don't speak Spanish?"

Buzzard watched Peggy's odd-shaped body slumped into a kitchen chair, her nose in the old accounts book. No wonder she had never gotten married, Buzzard thought. No man could figure her out—breasts too flabby, stomach stuck out, a thick neck, skinny legs. Rough looking, Buzzard thought. She was the kind of woman who could work like a man on the docks if there were ships around. She had never had a real boyfriend that he remembered, not counting Terry, a guy who looked like a circus freak.

Buzzard was sure if he hadn't lost his arm, he'd have a wife right now. His girlfriend had broken up with him before he got back from Korea, and Buzzard had never told anybody about the "Dear John" letter she had sent him while he was still overseas. He had made everybody believe she had left him because he was deformed without his left hand and would never be able to wear her wedding ring. "Women are that way," he said. "Crazy and always wanting somebody with two of everything, like they're so damn beautiful, for God's sake, when all the while they're hags in disguise." Buzzard had waged a battle on women since the "Dear John" letter, and he didn't have plans to quit. Now Peggy wanted to adopt an orphan from Mexico, and she'd be gone for over a week, and he wondered what he would do about cooking and cleaning, considering he only had one hand. Just like a woman, he thought, leaving when somebody needs her.

Peggy wore rollers in her hair the night before she left for Nogales. She wanted to impress the Mexicans with her wavy hair. She applied cream on her face that had an anti-wrinkle agent "guaranteed to erase wrinkles or your money back." Peggy didn't wear the face cream often, so she didn't know if it really worked. She thought of herself as someone the Mexicans would be proud to know, an American woman, who, by their standards, was rich. Never mind that she drove a beat-up old Dodge. It was better than taking the bus, which is what she thought they did. Peggy had the old Dodge checked by the mechanic down the street, and he filled the radiator up with coolant and told her he hoped she wasn't driving it all over town. He said the thermostat was almost gone, and she was lucky it hadn't blown altogether and caused the car to overheat. Peggy didn't tell him she was driving to Nogales in the car, as that would have made him take off his sunglasses and look at her as if she had just told him she had been driving the car around with sugar in the gas tank. She had seen that look before, more of a squint that told her she was the biggest fool he had ever seen.

PEGGY GOT UP EARLY on the morning of her trip. She listened to birds chirping and twittering, balancing on telephone wires outside her kitchen door. She packed her suitcase in the car along with the stuffed giraffe, the coloring books and crayons and plastic bags of old clothes donated by the church to give to the poor. She set up a Styrofoam water cooler on the back seat; everyone knew you didn't drink the water in Mexico unless you wanted to get the runs. In the gray dawn, she sat at the kitchen table drinking her coffee, taking in the stillness of the place and Buzzard snoring in his room. She took a bite of her toast and smiled. Pretty soon, she'd have her orphan; she could hardly wait to hold the child in her arms. She read over a passage from the Bible. *I came that ye might have life, and have it in abundance.* She thought, that was exactly what she wanted to give her orphan—an abundant life, something she had never known.

Peggy was ready to leave when Buzzard walked into the kitchen, still wearing his pajamas: white with a print of tiny, black bowling balls.

"Well, I guess you gotta do what you gotta do," he said. "What the hell? Somebody's gotta save the world. It might as well be my own crazy sister."

Peggy had just finished her morning prayers, so she didn't want to argue with Buzzard, as that would spoil the blessing of the prayer. She noticed he wasn't wearing any shoes, and he looked horrible in the early morning light. His hair was almost gone, and his teeth were yellowed by cigarettes and coffee. He slumped as he walked, his useless arm dangling at his side like a broken wing. The other hand ended in the shape of a claw, and his hunched back added to the appearance of a buzzard.

"Here," he mumbled, "you might as well take this. No telling what you'll run into adopting orphans all over Mexico. God knows if that old clunker will even make it."

He gave Peggy a hundred-dollar bill. For a second, Peggy wanted to hug Buzzard and tell him he was contributing to God's kingdom, helping her in her mission to the poor. She knew he didn't want to hear about God and missions, so she just said "Thank you."

"Well, I guess your hair looks nice," he said, and turned to go back to his room.

PEGGY LEFT PHOENIX and drove through a monotonous stretch of desert until she reached Tucson. She passed the town rather quickly and followed the highway leading into Nogales. The American side of Nogales looked like Phoenix or Tucson except for more billboards written in Spanish.

By the time she reached the border, Peggy's bad leg and hip were aching, a sharp pain reaching all the way to her ankle. She drove her Dodge into a long line of cars waiting for Mexican officials to check documents. She had heard of people held up by the *federales*, cars confiscated, people sent to a Mexican jail on suspicion of drugs or for not giving the right answers. Bribes were accepted, but had to be presented in a discrete manner. Peggy's head started to pound as she reached in her purse for two aspirins. She swallowed the pills with a cup of water she poured for herself from the water cooler. She had the signed letter from Reverend Cameron on the seat next to her. It was in Spanish and told anyone who read it who her contact was in Mexico and that she was a missionary worker for the Church of Christ in Phoenix, Arizona.

A Mexican official signaled for Peggy to put her window down and asked her in broken English if she was going to stay in Nogales or go further into Mexico. Peggy pointed with her finger at the ground. "Here," she said, "only in Nogales." She handed him the letter, and he looked it over. Her contact in Nogales was Luis Pacheco, a Mexican pastor.

"I know him. He know me," he said. He looked at Peggy, smiling, but didn't move. Peggy shifted in her seat, the pain in her leg throbbing. "You come out, yes, Señora?"

The man opened the door, and Peggy stepped out. Her bad leg gave way under her, and she stumbled forward. The Mexican official grabbed her and helped her stand up straight. Two Mexican officials watching from the entrance to the police station laughed out loud and asked the guy if she was drunk. He ignored them and told Peggy to open the trunk. He examined the plastic bags in the back, rummaging through the old clothes. By this time, Peggy was wondering if the car would be confiscated. She was already saying a prayer in her mind and reaching in her purse for money when he slammed the trunk shut and said, "We cannot keep Pastor Pacheco waiting." Peggy secretly thanked God she didn't have to pay a bribe. The man courteously opened the car door for her and waited patiently as she got in. He stood smiling, holding the door open in such a way that Peggy couldn't shut it. Peggy looked closely at him, reached into her wallet and took out a ten-dollar bill. He took it into his hand so quickly she didn't even feel it leave her palm as it disappeared into his pocket. All the while the man was gesturing with his free hand, as if he was talking to Peggy about the weather. He slammed the door shut and waved her through the border into Mexico. Peggy silently thanked God the man was satisfied with the ten dollars.

The streets on the Mexican side were crowded with cars and taxis, trucks and odd contraptions with no doors or hoods that Peggy couldn't identify as real cars. Curio shops, bars and liquor stores lined the busy sidewalks, and Mexican music blasted into the streets from everywhere. Men loitered on the sidewalks and at street corners, talking, laughing and smoking cigarettes. Kids jumped out at cars to wash windows. Vendors carrying blankets, hats, piñatas, fruit and anything else they could haul around in their hands or balance on their heads tapped on car windows every chance they got. Peggy smelled grilled meat, tortillas and beans cooking in pots. She figured the smells belonged to restaurants and houses built into the hills, some of them with gated entrances and stylish cars parked outside. This surprised Peggy, as she had thought that everybody in Nogales was a beggar. The rabble on the streets was just as Pastor Cameron had described, most of them beggars, sitting on dirt and asphalt. There indeed was stark poverty everywhere. Peggy was afraid to give any of them money. Once the giving started, she knew it would never end. She felt compassion rising like a small wave in the center of her chest, but in her throat, she felt something else: fear. There were so many Mexicans—some of them filthy and ragged—and she was alone.

Panic struck at Peggy as she maneuvered the old Dodge through the confusion of cars and people and remembered she had left the letter written by Pastor Cameron with the Mexican official. She wanted to turn around and go get the letter, but another car had already occupied the space she had left at the border. All she had was the envelope with the address to the church in Nogales. She stopped at a small café and walked in to get a soda pop, then decided to hand the envelope to the woman at the counter for help in finding the location of the church. The woman was two heads shorter than Peggy, her skin dark, and she had a red plastic rose pinned to her gray hair.

"¿Dónde?" Peggy asked, pointing to the address. Her heart was pounding, and her face felt flushed.

The woman spoke no English but was willing to help. She took Peggy to the door of the shop and began a series of gestures to indicate where the church was located. Peggy struggled to understand the woman, listening to names of streets and observing gestures indicating turns right, left and curves. It was useless, and Peggy turned to leave, her hip feeling like a hard knot.

The woman put her hand on Peggy's arm, and pointed to her leg. "*¿Dolor?*" she asked. Peggy knew the word meant, "pain."

"Yes," she said. "*Sí, dolor.*"

The woman walked to the back of the store and returned with a bottle of lotion she said was "*Buena.*" She pointed over and over again to Peggy's leg and then called a small boy who was walking down the sidewalk. She talked to him in Spanish, and Peggy knew she was telling him about her. She took the envelope and showed it to the boy.

He nodded his head; he knew where it was. The boy spoke in broken English. "Alfonso," he said, pointing to himself. Peggy walked out to the car with the boy and the bottle of lotion the woman had given her, relieved to have her own escort to the church.

IT TOOK THREE DAYS for Peggy to decide which orphan she wanted while she roomed in with the Pacheco family in a two-story house built on the side of a hill. Sewer water seeped out of pipes drilled into the back of the house, running down hard-packed dirt slopes, and Peggy worried because the water was forming stagnant pools filled with mosquitoes and flies. In the mornings, Peggy heard roosters crowing and chickens clucking. The morning sun rose, its light gently waking up animals and people. Peggy reacted to the early morning light with a bit of shock, realizing she was in another country, far away from Buzzard and their home in Phoenix.

Peggy found out there were rats hiding in the Pacheco home inside the cabinets in the kitchen; others were nesting in the walls of the house. The Pacheco kids set up mousetraps and were experts at killing the rats. Cockroaches, some as big as the ones Peggy remembered in New York, scavenged around in the garbage, and spiders wove fine webs in dark corner closets and along the outside of the house. The kids were fearless, stomping on the cockroaches and spiders, spraying them with insecticide. Señora Pacheco was skinny and tall for a Mexican woman—almost Peggy's height. She was quiet and barely raised her voice at her children. Pastor Pacheco was her opposite, fat and boisterous. Peggy could hear his heavy footsteps wherever he was in the house, and his booming voice traveled through every room.

The first night Peggy was there, she got sick on chili meat she had at dinner and had to keep running to the bathroom. She wouldn't drink the water and instead drank Pepsi or 7Up to ease her stomach. She cleaned the rim of the toilet seat every time she used it and swished the inside with a half-broken brush and disinfectant, watching for cockroaches that crawled out of the drain in the sink. Tears started as she thought of her own bathroom at home, and she found herself wishing she had taken Buzzard's advice and stopped herself from running all over Mexico adopting orphans.

PEGGY VISITED the orphanage run by the church, a stone structure set on the outskirts of Nogales. A colorful flower garden and groves of fruit trees filled with bright green parrots made the surroundings appear pleasant. The landscape was almost enough to make her forget she was in an orphanage. Later, Peggy found out the flowers and fruit were grown on the property to sell. The orphans were used as gardeners and fruit pickers. The place was run by a couple from the church, Edmund Wilson and his wife Elsie. Edmund was a jolly sort, from what Peggy gathered from those who knew him. On the day of her visit, Edmund was out at a ranch bringing in more orphans who had been reported living in a nearby cave.

To Peggy, the pastor's wife looked like she had contracted tuberculosis. Her eyes were sunken in and her bones stuck out. She invited Peggy into the living room at the orphanage, and immediately the room filled up with children of all ages. Elsie pointed to them listlessly. "Cute, aren't they?" Then she stood up, balancing herself on the chair's wooden armrest, and yelled at the kids in Spanish, barking out orders. The children scattered, and the women were left alone. Within five minutes, a young girl walked in holding a plastic tray with two cups of coffee, cream, sugar and sweetbread. The girl moved noiselessly and set the tray down on a small table between the two women. She cleaned each coffee cup off with a napkin, examining the cup carefully for any signs of stains. She then arranged the cream, sugar and sweetbread neatly for Peggy and Elsie. The girl's hair, dark and wavy, fell gracefully over her shoulders. Peggy was sure she had never worn hair rollers in her life. She smoothed down her own hair, conscious that it was straight now after two days' wear. The girl's face was like a pixie's, thin, her chin pointed, the eyes small, hazel lights. Peggy was impressed by the young girl's grace and asked her name.

"Oh, that's Emma, but she's not a good candidate," Elsie said and dismissed the girl with a nod of her head.

All day long the orphans clamored for Peggy's attention, hanging onto her hands and her pant leg, unbalancing her at times. Everywhere she walked, they looked at her; brown faces turned toward her tiny dark eyes, pleading. A chance to get to America with this gringa? Who wouldn't want that? Elsie told Peggy story after story of orphan tragedies. She spoke with little feeling.

"This one's retarded for lack of medical care at birth. That one was almost gone with dehydration when we found him. Most lost their mothers early on in life, and some have been raped, scorned, abused in every way possible . . . and there's more, lots more."

Peggy was tired, and she missed Buzzard, something she didn't think would happen. Listening to the orphan tragedies took what little emotion she had left. After three days in Nogales, she was sick of the food, the language, the smell of sewage and the constant movement of people in the house and on the streets. She was frightened not knowing Spanish and assumed everybody was laughing at her, maybe making fun of her limp. She finally settled on Emma, the young graceful girl who had served her coffee and sweetbread. Something about Emma—the look of total helplessness or maybe her blank stare—attracted Peggy. Pastor Pacheco told her Emma was not a good candidate. "She was a street child, a tunnel rat," he said. "She lived in the sewers under the city, between the United States and Mexico. She may have used drugs and may have been used as a child prostitute. Who knows?" He shook his head and sighed. "Not a good choice."

Peggy was shocked that a child like Emma could have been used as a prostitute, but Pastor Pacheco registered no shock. This was reality; he was not about to paint a pretty picture for Peggy. The more Pastor Pacheco told Peggy that Emma was not a good choice, the more determined Peggy was to adopt her. By the end of the week, the paperwork was finalized, and Peggy had permission from the Mexican government to take Emma Benites, eleven-year-old orphan, across the border as her adopted child. One year later, she would have to report on Emma's progress in the United States.

Peggy had envisioned adopting a younger orphan and now worried the stuffed giraffe and color books wouldn't attract Emma. She was wrong. Emma held onto the stuffed giraffe as soon as she saw it, and she took out the crayons carefully, one at a time, as she colored in the coloring book. She held up each crayon before she began using it, deciding where the color should go.

Peggy took Emma to a local store and bought her clothes and a pair of shoes. Emma was shy and unwilling to choose anything for herself. Peggy had to make all the decisions, and she felt she was giving Emma a head start on the abundant life by buying her new clothes. Mexican men stared at Emma, and Peggy felt uncomfortable. Emma ignored them all, talking to Peggy in whispers, walking close to her, sometimes reaching for Peggy's hand. Peggy wasn't used to being touched and found herself leaning away from Emma, making the excuse that her bad leg made her need more space.

Pastor Pacheco decided to throw a farewell party for Peggy and Emma, and his wife baked a cake with white icing and red and green flowers, the colors of the Mexican flag. "ADIÓS" was written across the top. The cake was sticky and sweet, the icing crusty. Peggy ate a piece and was glad the day of her departure was close upon her. She was tired of so many people, at the church and in the house. She was tired of the cramped quarters, no privacy and even Emma clinging to her.

On her way out of Nogales, the old Dodge started to heat up. Peggy turned into a gas station, and the mechanic told Emma in Spanish that it was the thermostat. Emma explained to Peggy in broken English that the thermostat had blown up and the car would burn up if it wasn't replaced. Peggy only had a few dollars left, enough to buy gas to get her back to Phoenix. Nausea struck as she thought she might have to stay in Nogales longer. Then she remembered the hundred-dollar bill Buzzard had given her. She searched for it in the tiny pocket of her purse. She handed the bill to the man, and he apologized, for he had no change for a bill that large. Peggy wanted to scream at him and make him go to a bank to cash the bill. It took all morning for the man to find someone who could break the hundred-dollar bill so he could repair Peggy's car.

A young man at the gas station tried to talk to Emma several times, and each time, Emma turned her back on him. Finally, he leered at her, and the owner came out to tell him to stop. "*Prostituta, puta,*" he said under his breath. Peggy wondered if Pastor Pacheco had been right all along in saying Emma wasn't a good candidate.

Before long, Emma disappeared, and Peggy looked for her frantically, up and down the street. She found Emma in the bathroom at the gas station, a filthy, fly-infested outhouse. She was sitting on the toilet fully clothed. When Peggy asked her what she was doing, she didn't answer. There was a part of Peggy that wanted to take Pastor Pacheco's advice and give up Emma on the spot. The girl sensed this and reached for Peggy. "Please," is all she said in a whisper. Her voice had no weight and disappeared as soon as the word was said. Peggy locked eyes with her, the girl's eyes shiny with tears, and she whispered back, "Okay."

The mechanic charged Peggy forty American dollars, and Peggy was unnerved. She knew this was highway robbery and that he had charged her a sum equivalent to four hundred Mexican pesos. She paid the man, lamenting the fact that Buzzard had given her a hundred-dollar bill instead of twenties. She looked around for Emma and saw her in the front seat of the car holding onto the stuffed giraffe and quietly coloring in one of the coloring books, ready for her trip to the United States.

BUZZARD WASN'T CONVINCED Emma's life on the streets was over. Mexican men looked at Emma with an interest not reserved for girls her age. Buzzard told Peggy not to bring Emma to the magazine stand. He had talked to a Mexican man who said he knew Emma's father in Mexico and that he was a drunken, violent man, wanted by the police for trafficking in drugs. The word "drugs" drove a stake into Buzzard's heart. He now felt as though Emma had made him and Peggy targets of a drug ring, mafiosos who had no conscience and no fear of the police.

"See what you've done for going around adopting orphans all over Mexico. Now we'll have to leave, and where will we go? I've told you a hundred times, one of these days I'm gonna go home. Maybe I'll do it now!" Buzzard remembered New York City, the Bronx, with no affection. Go back to what? All these years claiming he was gonna go back—a lie.

Buzzard talked to Pastor Cameron and told him Emma had to go back to Mexico. The pastor told him the adoption was legal, and it wasn't that easy to undo it. "Relations with Mexico are already strained," he said, "and I'm not one to bend the rod to its limits, so to speak. Keep the girl in the house so she can help Peggy. She can't cause any problems staying at home."

"What about school? She's in the sixth grade, for God's sake. Now what?"

The pastor explained to Buzzard that Emma wasn't going to school in Mexico, so it wouldn't matter, but Peggy had insisted that going to school was part of the abundant life, and she would not keep it from Emma. Buzzard didn't want to go into detail with Pastor Cameron about the possibility of Emma being a prostitute in Mexico. A child prostitute. Buzzard went through a mixture of pity and excitement when he thought about it. He wouldn't be able to explain it to the pastor. His heart raced, and he felt fully alive for the first time in years.

Buzzard never spoke directly to Emma. He didn't feel comfortable. He thought Emma knew too much; maybe she could see through his clothes, see him naked like one of her customers down in the tunnels. He didn't tell Peggy how he felt and went on ignoring Emma, which is what he did when he was afraid he might do something crazy. *Leave the craziness to Peggy.*

ONE NIGHT, Buzzard's house was broken into. Someone, a man, pushed his way into Emma's room. Emma escaped his grasp, running and screaming in her nightgown to Peggy's room. Buzzard got up and scurried around in his room, looking for his revolver. It was packed away behind one of his dresser drawers. He had to take out the drawer with his one good hand to find it. By that time, the guy was gone. Now Buzzard was mad, and worse still, frightened, but he didn't want to admit it. Maybe it was something related to Emma's past?

Buzzard broke his code of silence and asked Emma if she knew the man who had broken into her room. Emma said she didn't know him. Her face was pale, her eyes filled with fear. Buzzard knew she was telling the truth but couldn't say so. Instead, he yelled at Peggy, telling her that her clear conscience was gonna cause him to murder somebody.

After that night, Emma slept with Peggy in her room. She found the bottle of herbal lotion given to Peggy by the woman in Nogales and took to rubbing the lotion on Peggy's ailing leg every night. This made Peggy feel better, as she wasn't used to receiving comfort from anyone. Her leg didn't hurt as much, and she got closer to Emma. Buzzard took to wearing his revolver to work at the magazine stand, as men often appeared, and he knew they were hoping to see Emma. He felt like he was defending the girl from a pack of wolves. Rumor spread through the streets that maybe Emma had been brought over for Buzzard. It wasn't uncommon for a young girl from Mexico to marry an older man, even one old enough to be her father. Buzzard bore the stares of other men, some his own age. He wondered if they were jealous, and he was secretly proud they would think he could own Emma. The talk was so out of control that Peggy and Buzzard started getting obscene phone calls at the house.

By this time Peggy had enrolled Emma in school for the new school year, and Emma was elated. She could barely read, but Peggy had been teaching her, and every day, her reading improved. Buzzard was running around with a revolver at his hip, while Peggy was teaching Emma how to read. Secretly, Buzzard felt glad to see his revolver again. He had been a munitions specialist during the Korean War and was picked for the job because he feared nothing, or so it seemed. "Reckless" was what people described him as—"that crazy Buzzard"—except back then he was Steven Michael Wolf, US Army PFC. Now he was back to living on the wild side, having to protect Peggy and Emma. He had his own warfront all over again, and he didn't have to go to Korea to find it.

Emma never talked about her past life. She shunned all men and cut her hair like a boy and went to school every day. Peggy had her orphan, Emma had her family, and Buzzard had his war front. Peggy could have never figured this for the abundant life.

Bread and Water

When Gabriela heard the story about the woman who visited her husband in prison, she became frightened. Her aunt Tomasita, (alias Tía Tencha) said it was back in the old days, when snakes walked on their tails—before the flood. Her aunt paused for effect. "The flood. Remember Noah?"

Gabriela—tall with curly black hair cut to her shoulders, arms and legs too long for the rest of her body, nodded, "Yeah, I remember the story." In her mind she saw Noah and the ark in her old color book, a dot-to-dot picture.

"Anyway, this poor woman went every day to see her old man, who had been thrown into prison because he was found stealing clothes off a clothesline. Here he was taking all these clothes back home to his own children when a neighbor jumped him and wouldn't release him until the police came. Poor man! The lot of the poor to always get caught. I'll bet if he had been a Mafioso he wouldn't have gotten caught."

Tía Tencha straightened up from her work of peeling and cutting potatoes into pale, oblong strips that she rinsed in cold water and patted dry with a kitchen towel. She lined up the strips in bunches, raw french fries, waiting to be fried in hot fat.

Gabriela looked up at her from her task of lopping off the tops of celery sticks and chopping off the bottoms. She noticed facial hair below Tía Tencha's ears, stuck to her face with sweat. She watched her aunt run one hand quickly across her brow, sighing, "poor this . . . poor that," as she spoke. To Tía Tencha, everything was suffering in one way or another and was to be pitied.

"Well, that prison was not even fit for rats. That's the way prisons are in Mexico. So this poor woman would feed her man from her own breasts so he wouldn't starve to death! Can you imagine? He would suckle at her breasts like a baby! And while others died, he lived long enough to get out of prison and return home."

Gabriela looked down at the smooth, round lumps under her blouse, and a shiver ran up and down her spine. She could almost feel the horrible pull of a grown man's mouth and the biting of his teeth on her tender nipples. "Tía, stop it! What a terrible story! Bread and water—that's what they fed prisoners."

"Bread and water nothing! The firing squad is what they got and cockroaches for supper if they could catch them. What, you can't stand the truth? That is a woman's most perfect sacrifice—to give life, at whatever cost."

Gabriela was distracted from the conversation by a sneeze sounding at the kitchen window. Through the hazy glass, she saw Raul dragging a big branch to the alley. His lanky body was bent under the weight of the heavy limb, and his hat was stuck on his head like a cork ready to pop under the strain. Suppose I had to feed someone like Raul? The thought made her grip the knife tighter in her hand. A wetback, *un mojado*, just arrived from Michoacán. Maybe he has just been released from prison. Maybe he was the brother of the man who had suckled the poor woman's breasts. Maybe she should offer him a glass of milk before he got any ideas in his head. All these things went through Gabriela's mind as she tried to reason with the pictures Tía Tencha's story had painted in her head.

"You think too much," her mother always told her. "Stop thinking and start doing. A woman's work is never done."

"Here," Tía Tencha said, unaware of the impact her story had made on her young niece. "Take this to your mother, the poor thing. This soup will strengthen her. She's been so weak after this delivery."

Gabriela set the hot, steaming bowl of chicken soup served by Tía Tencha on a plate and folded two warm corn tortillas beside it. Her mother liked corn tortillas better than the flour ones. Pieces of chicken breast, seasoned to perfection, floated in just the right amount of rice, thick enough to blend in with every spoonful of the soup, yet not mushy.

Gabriela moved cautiously down the narrow hallway toward the last of three rooms where her mother lay on her bed with her third newborn son. At seventeen, Gabriela was the oldest of three boys and two girls, counting herself.

Gabriela walked in slowly, trying not to spill a drop of the soup. Her mother's eyes were closed. She was propped up on pillows, holding the newborn child to her breast. Gabriela looked up and noticed shadows of tree limbs forming dancing silhouettes on the curtains at the bedroom window. The wind was blowing outside, signaling a storm. She heard children's voices outside the window, calling to one another. The room was quiet except for the ticking of a clock on the dresser, an electronic heartbeat in motion.

Outside, the children's voices grew faint. The tree outside the window swayed wildly in the wind, its branches scratching the surface of the glass. Gabriela watched the tiny infant, suckling at her mother's breast in his sleep. "Mom?" she whispered. The bowl of soup trembled in her hands, and the spoon clattered up against the clay side of the bowl.

Her mother opened her eyes wearily and struggled to focus on her daughter. "Ay, Gabriela, you shouldn't have gone to all this trouble. I feel so weak. I can hardly think of lifting up the spoon to feed myself."

For one second, a horrible thought ran through Gabriela's mind. She wanted to grab the newborn, who was taking what little life her mother had left, and put him up to her own breasts. She was young, and she could take it. She'd sit with him in her own room and satisfy his hunger like the woman who fed her man in prison. Gabriela set the food on a small table next to her mother's bed, shaking off the image of her newborn brother suckling at her breast.

"Here, Mom, let me take the baby." Her mother released the baby carefully into her hands. "You're not on your period, are you? The forty days aren't up yet. I don't want him to get sick. You know I respect old traditions, women on their periods shouldn't hold newborns."

"No, of course not."

Her mother sat up to eat. As her mother ate, Gabriela rocked the baby carefully, back and forth in her arms, hoping he'd stay asleep. She noticed how big and heavy the baby felt, and then she looked at her mother's sagging body. It seemed a miracle that he had been able to fit in her shrunken stomach.

"Tell Raul to finish pulling all the weeds in the back yard. God knows he'll work from sun up to sun down.

He's such a hard worker. They all are, those *mojados*. Then give him something to eat."

Gabriela looked up in surprise. "What?"

"Give him something to eat. He won't hurt you. He doesn't want any trouble. The *migra*'s after him."

"Doesn't he have a home? A wife? How can you trust him in the house?"

"Maybe he's got one or two wives in Mexico. They all do. One in America, too, and kids all over the place. Still, he's a good man—a hard worker. Tell him I said to quit working. The wind's picking up. Look at the tree outside. There'll be a storm tonight."

Gabriela wanted to ask her mother if she knew the story of the man in prison who suckled at his wife's breasts. She stopped herself, as her mother didn't seem interested in anything. She didn't finish the soup, and leaned back on the pillows wearily.

"Mom, you've got to stop this."

"Stop what?"

"Stop having babies! Tie your tubes. God won't get mad."

"What will I tell God if I die after that? 'Oh, I had my tubes tied like all the crazy women nowadays. I stopped all the babies I was supposed to have from being born.'"

"He's not gonna ask you. He's got plenty to take care of as it is."

"You're not thinking like women should, Gabriela. Women have all kinds of problems—cancer and diseases of every kind. Why? Because they do unnatural things to their bodies. They go from man to man. They abort their babies and they never nurse, only stick bottles in their babies' mouths. And they wonder why they are miserable, why their lives are so sad."

"Isn't your life sad?"

"Of course it is, but at least I'm doing the right thing. My heart's at peace."

Gabriela lay the baby next to her mother. Her mother immediately closed her eyes and went back to sleep. Instinctively, mother and baby moved closer to each other, the baby snuggling, searching once again for his place at her mother's breast.

Gabriela heard Tía Tencha calling her from the kitchen. Before she reached the kitchen, she knew he was there. She smelled dry grass, leaves, dust, wind, sweat, and there was Raul without his hat on, sitting at the table eating a bowl of soup. He looked up at her and smiled. She noticed his eyes were blue, his skin turned brown by the sun. The nipples on Gabriela's breasts contracted, as if she was facing a draft of cold air.

"Use the celery you chopped up to make a shrimp cocktail for Raul," Tía Tencha said.

Gabriela turned her back to Raul as she worked on the wooden counter mixing tomato sauce, onions, small shrimp, jalapeños and the celery into a glass. Then she handed it to him without a word. She was grateful Raul stopped chewing as she set the shrimp cocktail at his side. She didn't want to see Raul biting into the celery she had chopped. He looked at her and nodded his head courteously, then turned back to his food.

"The wind is blowing hard. Too much dust," her aunt said, staring out the window. "There's a big storm coming. I'm leaving before it gets here."

THAT NIGHT, a storm ripped through the valley, knocking down power lines and picking up house trailers like they were boxes of matches. Gabriela's father set up candles in the bedrooms so the kids wouldn't be afraid when the power went out. "Raul has to stay overnight," her father told Gabriela. He was from El Mirage, which was at least sixty miles west. His ride couldn't get back to Phoenix because of the storm. "Raul can spend the night," her father said, as if he were talking about a child. "Tomorrow morning, he'll finish cleaning the yard."

Gabriela wanted to ask her father how old Raul was but didn't know how to do it. Instead, she asked, "What about his family? Won't they be worried?"

"They're all in Mexico. He's got nobody here. A friend here or there, cousins maybe. Maybe nobody."

"His eyes are blue. Why?"

"He's got more European in him, not so much Indian like me. I don't even shave! Raul's got beard all over his face."

"He's all dirty. How can you let him stay here like that?"

"Ay, Gabriela! That's enough! He can wash up. He's used to dirt. You take care of the kids and help your mom. I'm tired."

After dinner, her father went into the living room to smoke and watch television with Raul. They talked loud and fast, laughing about the boxing matches they were watching, exchanging stories about bosses and the gringos who don't know how to build houses like Mexicans do, and besides, that they get pushed around by their wives all the time.

"Gabriela, bring us some coffee!"

Her father's voice rose above the cheers of the crowd on television. Then, a loud clap of lightning sounded outside, and for an instant the house was immersed in bright blue light. The younger kids came running into the kitchen from their rooms and huddled around Gabriela, as if she could save them from being burned alive.

She hugged them tight. "Go back to bed, you'll wake up the baby and Mom." They heard the rain pounding on the rooftop, a deluge of water that seemed to have sprung from a waterfall in the sky.

"You kids get to bed!" her father yelled. "Everything's fine, ya, stop making such a fuss." Her father's words dragged out one at a time, his voice trailed, and Gabriela knew he was tired. He had worked all day supervising the work of a crew of men, mostly *mojados* who maintained the golf course at the country club. The grass had to be trimmed to perfection, and the sprinkler system had to work without a hitch, on time, every time. The men checked the system on weekdays when there were fewer golfers. Her father worked most Sundays as well, especially during golf tournaments. Then, he worked well after sundown, making sure the golf course was in perfect condition for the next day.

Once he had taken Gabriela to the clubhouse to wait for him while he rode a golf cart around, making sure each grassy mound was clear of debris. She sat in a small back room used by the workers and peeked into the huge lobby that faced windows spanning the sides of the building from one end to the other. The clubhouse boasted a fireplace as big as their whole bathroom with a mantle trimmed in gold. Plush carpet, a rich maroon color, spread luxuriously throughout the room. Armchairs and couches upholstered in satin blues and pinks looked so inviting she almost took a chance and ran in to sit on one. Her courage failed her when she saw white men sitting here and there, drinking, reading the newspaper, talking, some sleeping with their mouths open and their heads drooping. Through the windows, in the distance, she saw her father riding the golf cart, stopping every now and then to check a hole or a sprinkler. She went back to the room shared by the workers that faced huge garbage containers, lawn mowers, hoes, shovels and other tools. She put in two quarters to get a Coke from a vending machine. With the can, she toasted an imaginary companion, *salud*. She was a rich woman, sharing her favorite wine with her lover.

"Gabriela! The coffee! By the time this girl gets us the coffee, it will be morning!"

Gabriela heated up the coffee left over from dinner, adding a little water to it so she wouldn't have to make a new pot. She served it in fancy white china cups, not the ones the family used every day, and added sugar and milk, assuming Raul liked his coffee like her father did. She took the coffee cups into the living room, setting them next to the sweet bread on a flowered ceramic tray. Smoke from the cigarettes the men were smoking made the room hazy, and Gabriela felt as if she was walking into a dream. There was only one lamp on in the room, and outside the night was pitch black, the rain pounding fiercely against the windowpanes.

"Probably no work tomorrow, only at the clubhouse," her father said to Raul. "You should go by some day, Raul. I can ask the manager if he thinks there will be a job open soon if not there, at the other golf course. These gringos . . . own half the golf courses in Phoenix. They won't check your papers as long as you work hard and mind your own business." He yawned loudly.

Gabriela imagined Raul bending and stooping at the golf course, riding the big lawn mowers, trimming bushes, wearing a big hat to protect him from the sun. She stared into his blue eyes for just a second. The color was rich blue, like the flash of light that had broken from the stormy sky. There was a beard appearing on his face: she saw the stubble starting to form. He encircled the cup of coffee carefully in one hand. The skin on his hand was white compared to his face, the fingers shapely and slender and his nails dirty. He shuffled around on the couch, rearranging his long legs so he could balance the cup on his lap. Gabriela wondered about his height. All the other *mojados* she knew were short.

"Gracias, and I hope this isn't too much trouble, Gabriela." He said the words softly, pronouncing her name as if he was finishing a poem. Her name was the most important word in the poem, so he had saved it for last. She only nodded and looked again into the rich blue of his eyes, the dark pupils holding her gaze.

Her father took a drink of his coffee and changed the channel on the TV to the news. Raul leaned back and sipped his coffee, smiling. "Good coffee," he said. "The flavor is perfect." Gabriela knew he was exaggerating, but she smiled back and thanked him.

She looked over at her father, and he was already dozing off in his chair. He shook himself awake. "Bring Raul a pillow and a blanket—not a thick one. It's too hot for that. You might get a little cold," her father said to him. "We leave the cooler on all night. It's raining, but it's humid. Tomorrow it will be worse."

Gabriela searched in the closet for a blanket and found one that was thin and a bit tattered. It's probably better than he has ever known, she thought. She couldn't find a pillow for him, as they were all being used by the kids and her mom—even the baby had one. She took her own pillow, along with the blanket, walked back into the living room and noticed her father had gone to bed. The TV was turned off, and she could see the tiny ember of Raul's cigarette burning in the dark room. Before she reached him, he put out the cigarette in the ashtray. "Here's the blanket," she said. "And my pillow. That's all I could find for you."

"Take it back. You can't lay your lovely head on the mattress."

"You have to take it. My father will get mad if he sees I didn't get you a pillow."

Raul took the pillow from her hands and put it up to his face. He took a deep breath. "I'm in heaven!" he said, his voice thick with passion. "Your pillow smells like you."

Gabriela was glad the room was dark. He couldn't see her face turn red nor notice the chill that ran through her body, making her breasts tingle. Gabriela walked out without a word, thinking Raul had a lot of nerve talking to her like that.

SOMETIME DURING THE NIGHT, a loud crack sounded outside of the house. Lightning had struck, ripping off an enormous limb from one of the trees in the backyard. The crash of the fallen limb made it seem as if the roof had caved in. Gabriela woke up with the sound of the loud crack that was followed by the baby crying. She heard her father and mother talking, her father's voice loud, angry. She heard his steps in the hall, cursing because he had to go out in the wind and rain to see about the fallen limb. Maybe it fell on his neighbor's house or on an electric wire.

She heard Raul's voice, quiet, solemn. "Let me go out," he said to her father. "You stay inside. I'll take care of it. Leave it to me, por favor. Not another word."

Gabriela sat up in bed, waiting.

"Yes, como no," she heard her father say. "Here, take the flashlight. You're young and strong, only be careful. If it fell on the electric pole, leave it alone. The electric company will have to come by in the morning."

Her father trudged back to bed, his heavy steps more dead than alive. Gabriela heard her mother quieting the baby and the creaking of the mattress under her father's weight as he lay down. Gabriela got up and walked out after Raul. She was wearing one of her father's old T-shirts over a pair of shorts. She had given away all her nightgowns years ago to her little sister and had refused to buy more.

The rain had stopped, although the wind was still blowing. She stepped cautiously on bare feet, picking her way over the dark, wet ground. One lone streetlight was glowing, and that was the light she depended on to make her way in the dark. Raul was standing by the tree limb that looked like a massive wooden anchor sunk deep into the ground. Branches stuck out from it in all directions. Gabriela made out the outline of the severed limb in the dim light cast by a half moon that appeared to be racing across the sky. The wind was blowing dust, leaves and bits of dirt everywhere. She inhaled air that was heavy with moisture. Tiny droplets formed on her face, lips and bare neck. Raul was standing over the tree limb, his chest bare, his shoes on with the laces untied and still wearing his dirty pants. He was surveying the damage with the white beam of the flashlight.

"The moon's racing!" Gabriela yelled over the sound of the wind.

Raul looked up and saw her.

"The what?" Raul pointed the flashlight at her, momentarily on her face.

Gabriela was pointing to the sky, waving her hands. "The moon, *está corriendo*. She's racing!"

Raul waved his hands in the air, imitating currents of wind back and forth. His chest gleamed white in the darkness, and down the center, chest hair snaked its way to his waist and disappeared in his pants. "We'll never catch it," he said.

Gabriela laughed out loud, her voice disappearing in the wind as quickly as it had appeared. Raul was at her side, holding her hand. He reached down and picked her up in his arms. Gabriela smelled cigarettes on his breath, sweat, dust, wind and earth from his body. He was holding her close to his white chest, up against the black streak of hair. She was glad she couldn't see the color of his eyes in the dark. The stubble of new beard on his face scraped the side of her face.

"Put me down!"

"No!"

Gabriela started kicking until she unbalanced Raul, and they both landed on the grass. She scrambled to get up.

"Forgive me! It's all my fault!" he said, alarmed at seeing her on the ground. He brushed dead grass and leaves off her clothes, colliding with Gabriela's tender flesh under the thin T-shirt. "How stupid of me!"

He knelt on the ground, brushing the dirt from her legs, holding her close, and this time Gabriela didn't fight back. He pressed his head up between her breasts, breathing in deeply. The wind was blowing so hard it almost knocked them both to the ground. Gabriela was ready to scream, remembering the story of the woman feeding her man from her breasts. Raul placed his lips on one breast through her thin T-shirt, gently, tenderly, then on the next breast, his breath wet and warm. Gabriela's nipples grew hard, reaching for his lips. So that's how it happened —the feeding. The man's need, the woman's body giving. Gabriela reached down with her hands and encircled Raul in her arms, then forced herself free. Running back to the house she wasn't aware her foot was bleeding; she had been cut.

THE NEXT DAY, Gabriela's father asked her why she was limping. She told him she had stepped on one of the kids' toys in the dark.

"Be more careful," was all he said.

Even before they had had their morning coffee, her father and Raul were out in the back yard making plans to clear the dead limb that was on the ground. Gabriela's mother was up cooking breakfast for them. She was feeling better, she said. It was summertime, and the children were in no hurry to get up. The baby was sleeping peacefully in his crib, and outside, the new day promised a bit of sunshine. Her mother cooked eggs for the men, *chorizo*, with hot tortillas and chili. Gabriela looked at Raul once as he walked into the kitchen.

"Hello," she said in English, making herself foreign to him. He tried to imitate her.

"Halo," he said, glancing at her shyly.

Her mother laughed. "I sounded like that when I came over here years ago from Mexico."

"I'm not from Mexico!" Gabriela said angrily.

"Yes, but barely," her mother said. "She was born on this side of the border," she explained to Raul, "in Nogales. *Apenas*. We had just crossed the border. I was in labor, and my tía led me into her house, and right there in the poor woman's bedroom, Gabriela was born, on this side, *en los Estados Unidos*. Barely, she became an American citizen. I was lucky I was able to spend some time with my tía so I could register Gabriela's name in the court and get a birth certificate. We barely made it back over the line so her father wouldn't lose his job in the foundry. Remember, *amor*, how it happened?" She looked fondly at her husband.

"We were always in a hurry back then—in a hurry to get here, in a hurry to get back. Gabriela was born in a hurry." Her father laughed, Raul smiled and Gabriela walked out of the kitchen, limping.

RAUL WAS HIRED by the golf course; the gringos couldn't get enough help from the *mojados*. The golf course had to be kept clean and free of debris and, after the storm, there was much to do. Gabriela thought that if Raul was clean-shaven and well-dressed, he'd look like one of the white guys she had seen in the clubhouse. If he never said a word, nobody would know he was a *mojado*. Maybe she could meet him at the clubhouse, secretly. She'd get him a Coke from the machine and sit with him, toasting like they were two rich people taking their leisure, *salud*, staring into his blue eyes, the rich color of sky, and not letting him touch her—only look at her, his hunger never satisfied. That would be his prison.

Gabriela knew better. Her dad would get her to help Raul clean the clubhouse windows and vacuum the carpets, helping him move expensive furniture over the plush maroon carpet so he could be sure to suck up stray dirt into the vacuum. They'd be lucky if they could get a ten-minute break to drink a Coke.

Gabriela asked her mother where Raul planned to stay, and she said he'd rent a room from a neighbor down the street.

Her father glared at her mother. "No, he won't!" he shouted. "Raul will stay here with us. He'll be like my son."

Gabriela wondered what her father would say if he knew Raul had suckled at her breasts like the hungry man in prison, that he had pressed his mouth around his daughter's breasts and now was ready to spend the night with them again. Her father noticed nothing. He was surrounded by women and children who didn't understand him like Raul did. Raul sat quietly by, using his fingernails to scrape dirt off his knuckles. He was pretending it didn't matter to him where he stayed. Gabriela watched him closely and noticed there was a smile on his lips. She looked out the window at black clouds gathering as the sun set in a blaze of amber light.

GABRIELA'S MOTHER SAID THE STORM last night was bad, one of the worst she had ever seen. Maybe tonight there would be another one. The weather changed almost as fast as the human heart, she told Gabriela.

Spirit Women

It was like this the night the Spirit Women came to see me. The air was heavy, tipping one side of the world's scales until the whole thing spilled over and settled into my room, into baseboards, varnished trim and window panes. Things got tight around me, the thick air over me, a huge black crayon melting. I got tangled up in La Llorona's gossamer gown, the cry-baby, she-ghost, patron saint of weeping women: except that night, she wasn't crying. There were spirits of *malinches* there too, keeping La Llorona company—betrayers of men, women who would stick a dagger in a man's back as he slept. And other spirits, streetwalkers, notorious whores who did it with men for money, "riffraff all of them," my mother would say, "condemned to roam the streets at night and never be satisfied." And worse still—oh, much worse—there were women who had never been chosen, old maids who had never slept in any man's bed. Can you imagine never having been made love to, their flesh doomed to return to ashes and, who would care? Second wives, all of them; mistresses, all of them; spurned, all of them. Damn them all, their wounded hearts—my legacy!

Javier would say "It's all lies, Tonia. Your head is screwed on backwards. All you women are the same. That's the way it is. Life goes on." Javier washed his feelings away, like scrubbing his hands at the sink then looked at me. "You analyze things too much. Let's just enjoy the time we have together."

Sheets and socks held me tight. I slept in a faded, flimsy gown. It didn't matter anymore. I sat up in bed, leaned on my elbows, stared hard into the dark. The Spirit Women were on a mission. Crazy, all of them! Their eyes shifted and looked sideways at me, their arms folded around me like Gumby twisty-ties. They moved in shadowy dark spaces, electrifying the room with energy. Javier danced in my head, the fast dances, *cumbias, salsas, corridos.* He made my knees quiver, turned my socks wrong-side out and laughed because he knew I was watching him. The longer I watched him, the neater he got until every detail lay exposed under a bare bulb. His shirt was tucked in with no wrinkles, his pants neatly pressed, the crease perfectly marking the center of each leg. He was clean-shaven with a new haircut. Even his ears were washed red. Then he dissolved. He was too perfect for me. The Spirit Women pressed for details, all of them, the wretches, scrounging around in the air in a frenzy, wanting to put Javier back together again so I could finish looking at him once and for all; but I resisted, opened my eyes, rubbed the pupils hard to keep him from coming back. I disgusted the Spirit Women because they wanted me to be unafraid to see him at his best. That was the magic, to make me see him in all his perfection and let him go, but their magic was too strong for me. It made my head rattle and my fingertips get hot. The Spirit Women knew they were losing, and they couldn't take it. They weren't good at losing anymore. They whipped me hard with the tails of their gowns, put their fingers down their throats to show me how they felt. Then they vanished, and I was left alone. I crawled into a corner of my bed and shivered. The air had no weight again, and I was floating.

TÍA'S NAME IS AMANDA but we call her Manda—a promise, a pact between heaven and Earth—Manda. In my mind, I called her *Armada*, the Spanish warship, doomed to roam the ocean searching for English ships to destroy. Manda is Mom's sister. She came to visit on Monday, the same Monday I stood between a canyon's wall in a remote area of the South Mountains. It was important that day to shout. I declared it my shouting day—*el día del grito*. The shout was Javier's name and other names I learned to call him, curses all of them—so many curses I ended up spitting blood. The desert had eyes watching me. It answered me with hard, cold stares when I bounced Javier's name from one canyon wall to the other. All the vowels echoed together until they made one long sound that repeated itself like the drum of a passing parade. The louder I shouted, the better the chances he'd hear. The canyon walls held the pain of his name, neatly at first, then things got scrambled. I envisioned a landslide starting. I challenged the side of the mountain to roll on top of me, and I stood there, not caring, testing it, wanting to see a new landscape—distorted, twisted, imperfect.

"Good thing that rancher was out riding his horse that afternoon," my mother said. "What were you thinking? You could have died of heat stroke."

"Or a landslide," I said.

Tía Manda was sitting at the kitchen table balancing a cup of coffee in one hand. She looked like my mother, but her profile was softer, her eyes set farther apart. She wore dangling earrings that my mother hated and too much rouge. The pills the doctor prescribed for me made her face look fuzzy, her dyed black hair more frizzy. They were time forgetters. The pills sent me into a time warp. I walked dreamily through a place where earmuffs were in, and I wore double slippers on my feet. I talked softly and never shouted Javier's name. I didn't have the strength.

"Return her as soon as you can," my mother said. Her mouth moved in slow motion, and toast crumbs didn't disappear when she drank her coffee. Mom reminded me of an amoeba I had seen under a microscope in one of my lab classes. Everything about her was colorless, boneless, still-faced. Had she ever fought with a man like Javier? Not my father! He could never stand up to a battle. I imagined Mom immersed in an ancient sea—floating until she bumped into my father and swallowed some of the chemicals he was made of. The haphazard meshing of chemicals is how they became one. "The story of our lives," she would say. "That's the way it is. Why talk about it?"

I leaned my elbows on the table between my mom and my aunt and propped my face in my hands. Their faces kept slipping away from me like the handle of the cup when I reached for it.

I was a package getting ready for delivery. I saw "US Postal Service" stamped on my forehead and tattoos of strange-looking stamps etched on my arms and legs. Then I was whisked away in a huge cab I later found out was a Greyhound bus. No wonder the guy wouldn't let me out! I wanted to go back to the desert to finish the business of giving up Javier. I wanted to tilt my head up to the sky and burn my eyelids to a crisp. I wanted to let blisters rise on my skin like oily bubbles. I wanted to prepare myself to become a mummy. I'd find a crew of Egyptians schooled in the rituals of embalming and ask them to coil my body tight in linen wrapping so I couldn't escape even if I wanted to.

"I thought she was strong." I heard the words but couldn't remember who said them—not my kids. They knew I was strong. I kicked ass for them all through school, argued with teachers who picked on them, stood up for them when their homework was missing, defended them when I knew they were wrong. All three got my kisses until they were taller than me. I ruled over them—sometimes too hard—because I wanted them perfect. I wasn't; they had to be. Then I went off to nursing school and the sacrifices got bigger, the time I had left for family shorter. There were homework to do, tests to pass, school loans to pay. I was owned by the school and by Good Samaritan Hospital: everything had to be perfect. I graduated, an RN with honors. I was the cream of the crop for once.

I divorced Tommy one month after I graduated. The day the divorce was final, my mother served me a giant bowl of *albóndigas*, spicy meatballs swimming in a pot of boiled rice, oregano and garlic.

"I knew that man would be the death of you," she said. I wanted to tell her that I was the death of me, but couldn't imagine how I was dying. It was funny, really. I left Tommy behind, and all I could remember of him was that he liked apples. There had to be apples in the house seven days a week. My mother said my degree was enough, but it wasn't.

"Now you can get a good job, make good money, Tonia. You don't have to depend on a man—*brutos*, all of them!" My mother had an answer for everything, and I didn't want to confuse her in her old age. "Eat your soup, Tonia, it's getting cold! Who cares about that man? You gave your heart away and look what happened. You see?

All because you gave your heart away. Me—I hold onto mine."

"How?"

"How what?

"How do you hold onto your heart?"

"I just do, Tonia! I make myself not feel."

"That must be awful! I can't do that."

"You think so? You think that's bad? If you could see yourself now, then you would see what bad is. Who cares about love? It's just a word, something to say, a song you listen to on the radio. I stopped believing in that before you were born. Eat your soup!" Mom walked out of the kitchen without another word.

"It's not true," I said.

I saw the thin vapor rising from the bowl of soup, and the steam entered my nostrils, jarring me back to childhood, to a time Carrie and I played hopscotch until the chalk lines were only smudges and the sunlight had turned gray. Then we ran inside, arguing over who had won. On the stove was a pot of *albóndigas*, and we waited to be served, fighting over the same amount of meatballs. I lifted one on my spoon, draining off the liquid, then I bit into it to test for temperature. Carrie blew on hers first. She didn't take chances like I did. I didn't mind if I burned my tongue, as long as I ate one as fast as I could.

Was I a pig, greedy for life? For pleasure? If I had counted the pain, I would have never tried to tame anyone, except myself. I would have drawn the line between everyday horses and wild stallions and would have known that twitching tails meant more than skittish behavior. I should have recognized the signs that told me trust would never be enough.

"Most men aren't meant to be trusted," my father said right before I graduated from the eighth grade.

"Why not?" I asked.

He wound his wedding ring round and round his finger and looked past me before answering. "Men are like runaway horses. Half the time they don't know where they're going, but they figure they'll get there."

"What should I do?"

"First things first . . . don't chase them. They'll only run faster." I wondered if anyone had ever chased Dad. Mom never had. I knew she just let things happen. If he stayed, he stayed; if he left, he left.

By the time I started high school, that was my motto: *Don't chase them or they'll only run faster.* Maybe the right one got away while I was busy living up to my motto. Playing hard-to-get was confusing. I forgot my lines on a daily basis, and when my knees weakened around the star football player, I defied mushiness by holding my breath and then letting it out slowly from the corner of my mouth.

Tía Manda knew the truth I had stored in the canyon walls even before we headed for Ensenada after my mother told me for the hundredth time that Tommy would be the death of me. Tía looked right at me, that quizzical look of hers tilting this way and that to get at the truth. I shook my head ever so slightly, but it was enough. She knew it wasn't Tommy.

"I'll take her back with me," she said, nodding yes to my no. "She needs to hear the ocean. The kids will be fine. They can take care of themselves."

IT WAS EARLY SPRING. I was at Tía Manda's house. No one ever went there. It was so far away from Phoenix that I knew Javier would never find me there even if he had bothered to look. There were stories about Tía Manda, stories you stop telling when somebody else walks into the room. There was a man—no, several men—in her life when she was young. Married men? Yes, of course! Why would everybody need to whisper in the first place? Everyone said Tía had a screw loose, several even, but she was all I had.

Tía Manda's house was shaped like a crib. Its walls glistened in daylight with particles of sand and tiny seashells. Layers of ocean spray clung to the window panes, making the lamps inside the house look like they were under water.

I wallowed in the sounds the ocean made as it crashed on huge rocks during the day and splattered foamy bubbles up along the seashore at night. It oozed into my soul, hushing me, opening my ears to the breathy sound of seashells. The air tasted salty—so salty I didn't have to pretend I was spitting up Javier, nauseated by the smell of his kiss.

Tía Manda was a vision. Her frizzy hair formed halos over the lamps at night, and at sunrise, I smelled her salty body from my bed. She had lived by the ocean so long that her skin had turned crackly, and the creases between her wrinkles were speckled with sand. Her eyebrows reflected the uneven shoreline, admitting to expressions that blended with the smooth, rough spirit of the sea.

Monday was as good as Sunday for me. There was no clock in the room, no alarm to break the sanctity of morning. There was only a black tide ebbing inside me, water lapping over, sand shifting, footprints appearing and disappearing. This went on for days—hot, blazing days, wind-blown days that made the bones under my skirt stick out like handles. Still, I couldn't touch food. Every time I sat down to a meal, Javier showed up. He tipped the glass of wine and lifted it up for a toast. He sank his green eyes into mine. I was a cat, his hunter's prey, caught in the jungle of city buildings, blocked off in a corner of a nameless alley, unsnarling, powerless, my hands up over my head, my naked breasts exposed. His eyes devoured mine. I was convinced I owned part of him. Who was she, the other woman in his life, the dark bulk in my mind that Javier said could never be my equal? I didn't care. She didn't own him. It was me I saw reflected in his eyes. His passion reached for me across the table. I wanted to float over the top of the crystal and silver and land on his lap. Not kosher in a public place, I would imagine. And he laughed, his teeth perfect in the candlelight. I shuddered because even his hair reveled in the light, reflecting auburn gold, tiny stars that floated magically between us.

"Don't ever cut your hair," he had said the last night he held me in his arms. A Monday, a mundane Monday, the only time he could get away. He wound his fingers gently into my hair and kissed the long, dark strands.

"For you, I won't," I said, "ever."

IT WAS ANOTHER MONDAY when I finally opened my mouth to speak. By then my hair was cut so short I didn't bother to use shampoo anymore. I washed it with regular bar soap. Why waste the lather? My tongue moved in circles instead of up and down, defining the contours of my gums and palate, savoring the first syllable. Tía Manda dropped the book she was reading when she heard another voice besides her own. Timber, her Siamese, snarled from his haunt on the window ledge. He hadn't heard anyone else's voice except Tía Manda's for years. The sea lay before us, the sun behind us. I was held between two giants, Earth's forces pressed on either side. I was prey again, unsnarling, this time powerful. It was time to talk.

"His eyes were green . . . not the color of grass or trees," I said, "but green pressed on the surface of a mirror, reflecting light from underneath. If the petals of a rose were green, they would be the color of his eyes."

The strands of Tía Manda's frizzy hair stuck up in the wind, and she tilted her face my way but said nothing. She didn't even pick up her book from the sand. She sat perfectly still. The surf rumbled, the wind blew, a seagull called to its mate and the sun moved closer to the edge of the horizon. Colors played in the water. Blues and greens got all tangled up with one another, held hands, grabbed for heels, laughed and let go. The water sparkled with wavy circles, spirals that spun off the last rays of the setting sun.

"His teeth were perfect, and he smiled like a little boy. His beard grew every day, and his face was rough from shaving. The rest of his body was like silk."

The distant point of a sailboat came into view. I followed the tiny, white tent, so different from the colors of the sea. It bopped and chopped in the wind, catching drifts that brought it closer to home. I felt my mouth moisten a bit, and I licked my lips, smudging the salt-sea spray. The ache in the middle of my chest blazed, dying embers fanned by the windy surf. Someone (the Spirit Women?) took an invisible hammer and beat a nail into the very center of the biggest wound, and bloody foam gushed to the surface. Tía Manda saw it before I did, and from her perch on the wooden crate, she stuck out one leathery hand and put it on my arm. It felt strange to me, to be touched again, to feel the weight of another body on mine. I couldn't say another word. Javier was suspended in midair. He was dancing in the park with a white goose again while I looked on as he mimicked the swaying of the bird's smooth neck. He said the goose was dancing with him to keep him from chasing his mate, "like a man protecting his woman," he said. Javier was that way, inviting himself in, catching me by surprise, disarming me with absolute beauty. He did things to catch me off guard. He knew I liked to soar, to rise to the heights, even if it meant being dashed to the ground. He cradled my hand, his rough man's hand covering my own, the hard, worn surface blending atom for atom with the tender surrender of my own. The pressure of his arm next to mine was intoxicating. I inhaled the smell of his body, wanting more, greedy for the next breath.

I had reached perfection without trying. Javier was perfect. I was Eve watching my own Adam, newly born. I should have remembered there was a serpent in Paradise.

Wednesday reminded me—such an unremarkable day for a scheduled earthquake. Javier forgot to tell me she was pregnant. I had been transferred to obstetrics when she came in, ready to deliver the child he had lodged in her belly. She looked fragile, afraid, a young woman with dark hair pulled back in a ponytail. It was her first baby.

"Is there anything wrong?" asked Henrietta. "You look like you've seen a ghost." Henrietta, the nosy nurse who spied on me and listened through room speakers to find out what I was saying, saw through me.

"Stop imagining things," I said flippantly. I wanted to say "Mind your own business," but I knew that would put her on my trail for the rest of the night.

"There are donuts at the station," I said. "Better grab one before they're gone." Henrietta traded her sixth sense for the starchy pleasures of pastry. I let my breath out slowly from the corner of my mouth and rearranged my hair around my shoulders.

My skin prickled to know Javier was passing by, helping his wife into her room. He stood at her side as she lay on the bed, writhing in pain, his green eyes pleading with me not to tell, not to make a sign.

"You liar," I mouthed with my lips. I let my eyes penetrate his, unleashing my anger. She had run off with another man, he had said, probably in Australia by now. I fumbled around her bed, forgetting what I had to do, preparing for the birth, having to check her dilating cervix.

"You're so sweet," she said. "An angel."

Her weary eyes searched my face for the kindness a woman needs from another woman. I gave it to her. She really needed me. I managed my best smile over the point of her hard-packed middle. She received it and lay back, content to know the end was near. She rested quietly between pains, and Javier cradled her hands in his, the rough man's hands covering hers. Not once did he take his eyes off her to look at me again—not even when I held his son in my arms after the birth.

"Beautiful baby," I said.

"Looks like his mother," Javier said. He bent down and kissed his wife's damp forehead.

I must have closed my eyes, because when I opened them, it was nearly dark, and I couldn't see if the sailboat had made it home or not. Tía Manda's hand was still over mine, and she was gazing out to sea. She tilted her head my way, and her dark brown eyes stared into my own. It was the first time I had noticed anyone else's eyes except Javier's.

"He was married," I said. The surf hushed around us. Timber let out a yawn.

"I know," she said.

"I helped deliver his first baby."

The last of the sun went down. My face was wet. My eyes smarted. My hands were drenched. Did I dunk myself into the water? It took forever for me to get up, but when I did, my knees didn't quiver. My flip-flops snapped like rubber bands at my heels as I climbed the two wooden steps before I got to the door of Tía Manda's house. I was so sleepy I could barely put one foot in front of the other. I could think of nothing else but lying between clean sheets, lulled to sleep in my own cocoon like a caterpillar waiting for the right time to emerge. I smelled Tía Manda's salty body at my bedside. Her sandy hands brushed over mine, tucking the sheet neatly under my chin. She bent down and kissed my damp forehead.

That night, the Spirit Women visited me again. I hadn't seen them in months. I wasn't surprised that their spirits found me at crazy Tía Manda's. She was one of them. They crowded around me in filmy, compact layers to see if I looked like them. They compared battle wounds with me, searching out the deepest wounds, baring their breasts and backs to show me the wounds of loving a man who couldn't love back. I remembered my motto again: *Don't chase them or they'll only run faster.* I smiled, then remembered I had forgotten how to laugh. I made a few noises that sounded like laughter, and it was enough to get the Spirit Women started. They giggled like schoolgirls, translucent shoulders jiggling, hands up to their transparent lips. Dissolving the compact layers of filmy atoms, the Spirit Women linked hands, playing ring around the roses, making a huge white halo all around the room. They pranced so fast they turned into ashes landing in a heap, tangled in their own spirit gowns. They sprinkled some of their ashes on me, on the deepest wound, sealing it in just the right places. It felt so good not to ache anymore—not to want anything.

Ol' Lady Rentería

A bsolutely, yes, you will succeed. It's written in the stars, told to you by Ol' lady Rentería who owned the house with a hole in her bedroom window stopped up with newspaper. Ol' Lady Rentería was strange. Some said she was a witch—the neighborhood witch who killed her husband and God knows who else. Her potions were flying in the air around her house, thick as a horde of gnats hexing everyone within arms' reach.

We hid in the hedges, Chan and I, and got pollen dust all over our hair from the flowers that bloomed between the green, glossy leaves. We hid there to spy on the house before we got closer. We watched for movement at the windows but saw none. Ol' Lady Rentería's husband had died by then. Some said she had poisoned the ol' wretch with oleander leaves she crushed and made into a powder. She sprinkled the powder into his coffee and on his refried beans. He never noticed, the old drunk. How could he? He drank a pint of whiskey every day. He deserved to be poisoned, the old bastard. It didn't matter to us. He wasn't around anymore to sic his dog Víbora on us and make us pay for stealing his peaches. I hated that dog. I was glad when one of the neighbors fed him a poisoned piece of meat. The ol' man and the dog died around the same time, of the same symptoms, and good riddance to both—victims of one of Shakespeare's modern-day tragedies.

I remember the day Ol' Lady Rentería told Chan his fortune. It was sunny and windy at the same time. Branches of huge tamarisk trees were peacock tails fanning themselves to life with every gust of wind. Dust devils swirled around corners of telephone poles, looking like silhouettes of La Llorona, the weeping woman, the gruesome child-murderer we were mortally afraid of. There she was . . . there, there and there, now brushing close to us, now laughing, her teeth forming huge black gaps. She'd wait until it got dark. Darkness was her cover. That's what scared me—that she never came out in the daytime when we could see her. It was always at night when her cold, hard fingers could trap us forever.

We couldn't keep the powdered Kool-Aid from flying off our hands and had to keep sticking our fingers into the packet to reach for more. We mixed the powder with sugar and made it taste like candy. Chan's lips were purple; mine were red. We smiled anyway because the colors were so delicious. We smacked our lips, and the one who smacked the loudest got to ride the bike the longest. My hearing was better than Chan's, but he cried louder, so I had to give in every time. That's the way it was for me, always giving in to Chan, making myself weak so he could be strong.

"Let's knock," Chan said.

"She's not home," I answered.

"Where would she go? She can barely walk."

Chan was right, even though he was in fourth grade and I was in seventh. I was dragging my feet all the way up to her kitchen door. We knew she never opened the front door. There was a bureau pushed up against it as ancient as she was. No one knew if the front door had ever been opened. Some people said the bureau was really a coffin with dead bones in it, the bones of Ol' Lady Rentería's mother and father.

The Rentería kids crawled in through a hole in one of their bedroom windows when Ol' Man Rentería locked them out—all nine of them, locked out and sitting around in the back yard until he decided to let them back in. One night he forgot they were out there, and they ended up making beds out of huge splintered boards. Pilar from next door gave them some blankets and a couple of flat pillows. Ol' Man Rentería made her take them back. She threatened him with the cops. Rentería's oldest daughter, Soledad, got down on her knees and begged Pilar not to call the cops because he would kill their mother. And that's the way he kept them in line. The truth was, Ol' Lady Rentería died the day she married that bastard.

Another reason I didn't want to go into Ol' Lady Rentería's was that Soledad told me her ol' man peed everywhere like a dog, like Víbora, except he didn't lift his leg. I couldn't believe it until the day I smelled the soles of little Ana María's shoes, the littlest Rentería, and they smelled just like pee. She said she had stepped into one of her father's puddles. The puddles would be dry by now—it had been three years—but it was the principle of the thing that bothered me.

Chan knocked on the greasy door. Really, we could have given it a little push and fallen into the kitchen because it was that rickety. The word "voodoo" came to mind. The vision of a fallen world flashed for a second before me—a world where goats were kept as pets and fed cornmeal through their horns, a world where hearts of dogs and cats simmered in blackened pots. I imagined the animal organs frozen in clear plastic bags, waiting for a ritual to begin. The house's rooftop had a jagged twist at the tip, like the devil had sat on the top and made himself at home. The house was so scary kids wouldn't even trick-or-treat there on Halloween except on a dare. The kids said Ol' Lady Rentería prayed to the devil, Satan himself, horned, hoofed, the whole nine yards. "You can tell," they said, "because she smells like ashes and sulfur, which everyone knows is the smell of hell." If someone died unexpectedly, people wondered if the cause was due to one of the ol' witch's spells. Healthy today, gone tomorrow —it was foul play for sure. Chan said it didn't matter: he was an altar boy, a real altar boy wearing the holy robe on Sundays and on Halloween nights as a disguise. Chan carried a plastic bottle of holy water when he went trick-or-treating at Ol' Lady Rentería's. He sprinkled it on the old lady's property, one sprinkle at each corner of the lot, running so fast he was a blur in his holy altar boy robe.

Two of Ol' Man Rentería's sons were in prison, and another had been shot in the mouth by his wife who said he deserved it for kissing other women. Eventually, Soledad became a half-person, living in a residential home for the homeless. I saw her once, smoking cigarettes on the corner of the street, dressed in faded jeans and a blouse with Mickey Mouse on the back. She had been married three times and had at least six kids, two from each man, although none of them were twins, but all that came later, much later.

The day Chan knocked on the door, the younger kids had gone over to the canal to play. I didn't really see organs simmering in pots, but I thought I smelled a bitter odor, even before Ol' Lady Rentería opened the door.

"Need anything from the store?" Chan asked her, not that he cared. He wanted in. That's the way he was, always pushing his way in where he knew he shouldn't go, ready to brandish his smile like a banner that would sink the most hardened woman's heart.

There she stood . . . cough, cough, cough. She was coughing and not covering her mouth. I stepped back, afraid she'd contaminate me with TB germs. Her white hair was wild on one side, plastered down on the other. Her bottom teeth were missing, making her lip droop. There was a tattoo on her nose that everybody said she had done to herself because she belonged to some crazy cult that put a brand on their noses to prove they had the power to sniff out a person's personality from afar. She looked at Chan and smiled like she had been expecting him all day.

"Come in, Darío." It sounded so formal, his name. I never liked it. I called him Chan, to this day Chan, even though now, of course, he'd die if I called him Chan in the company he runs with.

What about me? I thought, Ol' Lady Bruja. No welcome for Mercedes? But she wanted Chan—led him like a sleepwalker to the kitchen table. She wore cloth slippers that looked like dead Easter bunnies on her feet. Her dingy brown blouse was transparent but showed nothing at all, certainly not anything that resembled breasts. She was covered in part by a cowboy vest that lifted up in the back to outline the hump on her back. Her black skirt went down to her ankles and hardly moved at all when she walked. Was she walking or flying through the air? I couldn't tell.

Chan sat down with her on a couch covered with a rumpled bedspread, faded in some places, threadbare in others. It was an opportune time to talk, just the two of them. I was helpless to say a word. A shield rose up around Chan, securing him to her. I couldn't see it, but I could feel it, every molecule of it, hardened, transparent.

I was shut out. I couldn't even open my mouth. What had she done to me? To this day, I don't know.

"Darío, you will be a great man, one in a million, next to none. No one will be able to catch you. You will be a comet passing by, lighting up the sky like a firecracker. And you must be ready!" I saw Chan smile, the alarming, wondrous smile that was his very own—chin up, huge, broad, gray eyes filled with the look that said he was already twice his size, a famous movie star, a leader of nations, a wealthy man.

Then she whispered something I couldn't hear. Only to Chan did she whisper, and he listened intently, cocking his head to the right. I wanted to yell, "It's a lie!" but I couldn't make my lips move. She put her hands on Chan's shoulders like everything was settled and he was her knight going off to battle. I tried to reach for Chan, to drag him out by the arm, but I couldn't touch him. He was behind the shield—her possession. She looked at me, then away, down at Chan, over his shoulder back at me, then she looked like an idea had just gotten into her head. She opened her mouth to speak, then decided not to tell him anymore. It was over, whatever it was.

"Yes, Darío, what a beautiful child, dark curls, gray eyes, more beautiful than all my brats put together!"

"YES, I know there's static. What do you expect? I'm flying over Mexico City. You're such a complainer, Mercedes. Stop fidgeting. I know you're curling the phone cord in your fingers."

I opened my mouth to say something, then shut it, trapping my thoughts like Ol' Lady Rentería had done when Chan and I were kids. I was weary suddenly, not knowing how to convince Chan that something was good for him. Life is like mercury flowing. It slips through things, a thin stream, reflecting everything, dangerous as it passes by. Chan knew too much not to be home when Mom was on her deathbed. "She knows I love her," was his excuse. He spoke to her by phone. She was unconscious.

"She hears me," he said. "Why not? I'm her only son."

"She needs you now!" I yelled.

"Don't get flustered. I have to finish this deal. It means millions. The stock market would stand still if those high rollers knew the details—stand still, dead in their tracks. Mom would say stay."

"Because that's what you want her to say. She'll do what you say."

"And you, Mercedes? Will you do what I say? Get off my back. Settle down. I know what I'm doing."

It was useless. His mind was a closed trap. There was one person inside—himself.

"That ol' lady made you rich, Chan. Nobody could ever tell you what to do."

"What old lady?"

"Ol' Lady Rentería. She made you what you are now. Don't you remember when we were kids? She told you your fortune, filled your head with all kinds of crazy ideas. Sent you off to become, what?"

"Are you talking about Soledad's mother? Ol' Lady Rentería! The poor old lady the whole neighborhood was afraid of? Everybody treated her like she was the neighborhood Llorona, for God's sake."

"Poor old lady, my ass! She was a witch! All you have to do is look at yourself to see what she made you into."

"Nobody made me. I made myself! Get it straight, Mercedes. The more you have, the more you get. It's the law of supply and demand. The more the demand, the more I supply."

"Yeah, until there's no room for anyone else but you."

"I'm self-sufficient. Nobody helped me, much less Mom and Dad.

"That's the biggest lie I've ever heard. What are you, nuts and bolts? Inhuman? Never mind about coming home. Mom just died."

SOLEDAD KNOCKED on the door the day Mom died.

"I heard," she said. "I'm sorry. My mom's been gone so long, I forgot when she died."

I didn't want to tell her I thought her mom was a witch who had cast a spell on my brother. All these years held in the power of Ol' Lady Rentería, my brother Chan, who had no feelings for Mom as she died.

"Thanks for coming by." Soledad sat around in the living room with aunts, uncles and cousins. There was a twig in her hair, flakes of dried evergreen leaves. "I've been working out in the yard," she explained.

The Rentería house was changed. Remodeling had occurred. After Ol' Lady Rentería's death, Soledad moved in with one of her boyfriends and the kids that looked like twins. The crazy twist on the rooftop had been straightened until it was flush with the rest of the roof. The oleander bushes had been cut to bare stems and thick, short trunks. Windows were patched up, the front door opened and the kitchen door was just a kitchen door. The antique bureau had been thrown out into the alley, and the Zúñigas had picked it up because they were poorer than the Rentérias. Where had Soledad put the bones of her grandparents? I didn't have the heart to ask. And the pot where the old lady boiled the entrails of animals? Was I believing a fairy tale? A witch story? A rumor?

"Why isn't Darío here?" she asked me.

"He's on his way."

"From where?"

"Flying over Mexico City—la capital. He's a big businessman, you know. Doesn't think it's important to be home when his mother's dying."

Tears came down my face in a flurry. They had been waiting there for over twenty years. I couldn't stop crying. Aunt Flora held me in her arms. Cousin Hilario sat with me on the couch, and still the tears went on. By this time Soledad was crying, too. A floodgate had been opened between us. She sat on an armchair, and I sat on the couch, and every time we looked at each other, we cried all over again.

"Your mother was a witch!" I said, sobbing so hard Soledad couldn't understand a word I had said.

"A what?"

"A horrible witch! She put a spell on Chan, made him her puppet—over at your house when we were kids—a puppet, an empty shell!"

"My mother? A witch? What about your mother? She always thought she was so good, so holy! Did she ever invite my mother to your house? Did she ever treat my mother like she was human?"

I was on my feet. "*Was* your mother human? Don't you know all the stories? She killed your father, for God's sake! Even though the bastard deserved it—didn't you know?" My voice was coming from my gut, deep ripples of sound that crashed from my throat and made everybody rush into the living room to see what was going on.

"I think you better leave," Hilario said to her.

"I'm not going until she apologizes to me for saying my mother was a witch and she killed my father."

"I'm calling the cops," Hilario said. "We don't need this shit around here today."

"Don't! Hilario, don't call the cops Mom just died. I don't want cops over here."

"I'm not going until you apologize to me," Soledad said, pointing at me. I noticed her jeans were cut unevenly at the knee, and strings of the fabric hung over each leg. She looked so defenseless. Her feet were stuck in dirty flip-flops worn to a thin edge at the heel.

"Get out, you bitch!" I sprang at her before anybody could stop me. I hammered my fists into her face, her breasts and her belly. I wanted my brother back; I wanted my mother back. How dare her witch of a mother change things—put dark spells on everybody and make them crazy for the rest of their lives. Somebody had to put things back in order again and rid the air of the hexes, seal the boxes shut. Hilario pulled me from her and held me in a tight grip.

Soledad stood looking at me, her nose a bloody mess. "My mother was no witch! She was a lonely old woman that nobody ever cared about, including my father. Your brother went gay—that's what happened. Gay, and your father hated him! Admit it!"

"Liar! Liar, liar—all lies!" Even as I said it I knew I was the liar. All these years lying to myself, blaming Ol' Lady Rentería for the secrets I couldn't bear to tell myself.

"Get out!" I shouted.

"Not until you apologize!"

"I'll get her out!" Hilario said. He went toward her, ready to pick Soledad up and throw her out the door.

Soledad's blouse was torn at the shoulder. A red bruise on her skin showed up through the tear. There were always bruises on Soledad's skin. I had forgotten—bruises. Who hurt her now? Her father was dead. It was me. I did it.

There she was, Soledad, shaking and shivering with rage; Soledad who slept on boards when her father locked her out of the house; Soledad who begged Pilar not to call the cops because her father would kill her mother; Soledad who married drug addicts and had to raise their children alone. Where was my mercy, my compassion? Maybe the spell had been cast on me. "Let her go," I said.

"Darío is gay, Mercedes," she said in a matter-of-fact tone. "You know that. My mother was the only one who ever had the guts to share the truth with him, to look into his heart and tell him it was okay. It wasn't a witch's spell she cast on him. It was the truth, and if you think the truth is so bad, try to live with what your brother's been through. All of you wagging your fingers at him, laughing at him, talking behind his back, eyeing him like he was an alien from another planet. You drove him away years ago."

"It's not true."

"Yes, it is. It is and so what?" Soledad looked right into my eyes, unswerving. I was in a time capsule. Everything had stopped all around me—conversation, kids, the clattering of coffee cups, all silenced.

"And you knew?"

"Your brother visited my mother lots of times, not just once."

"Why didn't you tell me?"

"You didn't want to know."

Flora's newborn baby cried from the bedroom and the sound made us all move at the same time—a picture unfreezing.

"Mom wasn't a witch. She just wasn't afraid of the truth, and if she killed my father, well, that's too bad. He deserved to be dead."

"That's cold-hearted!"

"Not if you knew my dad."

"Go wash your face. It's a mess . . . and I apologize."

"Don't apologize, Mercedes!" Hilario said. "What are you, crazy? She's got her nerve coming in here telling you all this on the day your mother died."

"It's the truth. What am I supposed to do, act like it's not? Right, Hilario? It's the truth, isn't it?"

Hilario turned and walked out the door. If I remember clearly, Hilario was the one who wanted to beat up my brother one night after a party. I never found out what they had been arguing about. I wondered if it had anything to do with Chan's friend, Cipriano, short, feminine-looking, his hair grown out to his shoulders and dyed blonde. Chan brought him over sometimes, and Dad threatened to throw him out each time.

A thin mist gathered in the air. I brushed my hand over my face to dispel the cobwebs. I figured the spell had just been broken, the one that held me at bay, one step behind my brother's life, never knowing how to talk about it, how to answer all the questions, afraid if I asked too much I'd find out things I didn't want to know. How could my brother be so masculine and turn to other men? Was it a gene gone crazy in our bloodline? Maybe he hated my dad's guts and turned to other men to get revenge on the whole macho race. The word "lovers" made me think of porno magazines, men posing with other men, women posing with other women, anal sex, oral sex. My brother the pervert, a *joto,* one of the worst things you can call a man in Spanish. How could I have sat with Mom at the breakfast table, the place we talked together about everything because we were still half asleep and didn't know any better and told her, "By the way, Chan is a fag. He'll never have grandchildren for you. He'll die in the arms of another man and never carry on our family name. And me? I'll sleep with my husband some day, and while I'm making love I'll wonder what Chan is doing and if it's the same for him or different—the feeling of having sex, of getting lost inside somebody else."

Suddenly, there was something I had to do, but I couldn't remember what it was. I grabbed Soledad's hand, pulled her into the bedroom and started handing her clothes—a blouse, jeans, a pair of sandals. "Here, take it all."

Flora stared at me. "What the hell's wrong with you?"

"Nothing."

Soledad looked up at me and smiled. It was the first time I had ever seen Soledad smile.

CHAN CAME IN on the 11:00 pm flight with a man he said was his assistant—Eric, so good-looking, I blinked hard to keep from looking at him too long. I reached for Chan and hugged him, held him close, caught the sweet scent of his aftershave. I held him, and we cried together.

Eric adjusted Chan's leather carry-on onto his shoulder. Now he had two carry-ons, one on each shoulder. He was a human fulcrum, balancing weights. We walked through the airport crowd, Chan and I, with our arms wrapped around each other, Eric swaying with the carry-ons. Dimensions opened before us. I sensed Mom close by and Ol' Lady Rentería, unmasking us—turning her spells inside out so I could look at them.

Confession

Big Boy's real name was Edward Ornelas, but nobody ever called him Edward, because by the time he was ten, he weighed in at over 150 pounds. He lived south of Van Buren, in the Marcos de Niza Projects, close to the neighborhood where the girl had disappeared the previous October. Big Boy lost twenty pounds once he was put in juvie at age eleven for shoplifting at Woolworth's, taking things he could have bought for nickels and dimes: Batman and Robin plastic figures and a Batman car. The reason he got a term at juvie was because one of the clerks said he had seen him several times lifting things but couldn't prove it, so due to suspicious behavior and to teach him a lesson, he was given six months at Boys Ranch.

His mother Luz, who subscribed to the *Catholic Monitor* and attended meetings of the Sodality of Mary at St. Anthony's, was so ashamed of him that she wouldn't visit him while he was in juvie. She had the entire church pray rosaries for the salvation of his soul and had a photo of her son set up on her dresser with a candle burning in front of pictures of saints and one of St. Michael the Archangel with his foot planted on the devil's neck. Luz's sister,

Nena, who didn't subscribe to the *Catholic Monitor* and couldn't have cared less about sodalities or saints, went to see him with her daughter Atalia who was a sophomore at Phoenix Central High. Atalia insisted that Big Boy was innocent of stealing the Batman and Robin figures and had been mistaken for another boy, a huge Indian kid nicknamed Squirt.

"He didn't steal a thing!" Atalia told her mother as they drove to juvie to see Big Boy. "All he had in his pockets were toothpicks and bubble gum. That guy at the store had it in for him. He's always watching the Mexican and black kids. I tell you, this time it was an Indian kid . . . I saw him. Big Boy's nothing but a crybaby. He's probably crying every night in juvie. We should talk to the judge."

"Never mind," Nena said. "Nobody will believe you. Just leave it alone. He'll be out soon."

BIG BOY WAS FREED from juvie exactly six months later, thinner, sullen and "reinvested in his life," as his probation officer, Howard Franco, described it. "Done his time," Franco said at the court hearing. "Now he's ready to take his place in the community, finish his eighth grade year and move on to high school. Right, Ornelas?" Franco never called him Big Boy, as he didn't think kids should be identified by anything except a number or their last names.

Luz was there, sitting next to Franco, watching her son one chair away from her. Her eyes filled with tears as she thought of how thin Big Boy had gotten. Maybe she had been too hard on him. After all, he had always been close to her—maybe too close. She worried he didn't like girls, and now she worried maybe he had a boyfriend in juvie. She worried boys his age wouldn't be stealing Batman and Robin plastic figures, and maybe his cousin, Atalia, had been right in the first place—the store clerk had it in for him. She cursed the day Big Boy's father, Edward Sr., had walked out on her to get together with an older woman—a bar maid from the American Legion Hall, the place that boasted a dark, musty bar where Edward Sr. drank himself into a stupor every Friday night. Her boy needed a male figure in his life, she reasoned, and decided to call up Father Leo at St. Anthony's, the most saintly man she knew, to stand guard over her son's life.

FATHER LEO HAD A HUGE BALD HEAD and a smile that went from ear to ear when he was in a good mood. When he was in a bad mood, he shook his fist at whoever happened to stand in his way, assuring them they were all headed for hell if they didn't take their religion seriously. He could be seen at night walking up and down the sidewalk in front of the church, reciting litanies to honor saints and supplicating for the souls of his disobedient parishioners. It was rumored he had a crucifix in his room with a Jesus hanging on it with real glass eyes that shone in the dark and kept Father Leo company as he lay on his bed, some said, "weeping over the sins of the world."

When Luz approached Father Leo about taking Big Boy under his wing, he told her he would hear his confession, then Big Boy would have to pay the two-dollar fee so he could join the St. Anthony's Boys Club. Most of the club members were altar boys and were also part of Father Leo's baseball team. Big Boy wasn't athletic, so he told the priest he'd rather be an altar boy and not play ball, and the priest told him confession was the first requirement for becoming an altar boy, as boys with ruined souls were unacceptable.

In the dark box that represented the confessional, Father Leo heard Big Boy's confession one Saturday afternoon, with two skinny girls and their grandmother waiting in line outside the thick curtain that covered the doorway of the confessional. The confessional opened first to one side, then the other, as Father Leo slid open the small screened panel. Waiting in the dark, Big Boy's legs felt like two iron rods glued to the vinyl-covered kneeler with its seam ripped open on one end.

The screened panel opened with a sound that made Big Boy jump, and in the dim light, he saw Father Leo's profile leaning up against the wire mesh.

"Bless me, Father, for I have sinned." His mouth went dry as he fumbled for the rest of the words. "Ah . . . this is Big Boy."

"Don't tell me who you are!" said Father Leo impatiently. "You're a sinner—that's the only important thing. God doesn't care about anything else." On the other side of the thick curtain, Big Boy heard one of the skinny girls laugh, and he wondered if they were standing close enough to hear what the priest had said. "Now tell me the truth . . . did you shoplift at Woolworth's? As you know, 'Thou shalt not steal' is one of the Ten Commandments."

"No, Father, I didn't steal, but I wanted to . . . sometimes."

"Well, wanting to, is just as bad as doing it. You have to live clean from your heart. The devil wants your heart. Don't you understand?" Then there was a pause, and Father Leo got close to the wire mesh screen. "Never mind about Woolworth's," he whispered. "What about that girl who disappeared last year? What do you know about her? She was one of your friends, wasn't she?"

"Who? Nanda?"

"Yes, Nanda. I know how you boys looked at her . . . and now she's gone."

Big Boy's face got bright red in the dark confessional. He felt hot and shuffled on the kneeler. He knew who Nanda was; all the boys did. She wasn't afraid to let the boys touch her breasts—two huge mounds that grew on her chest—on summer nights at Harmon Park. Usually one of the older boys would end up taking Nanda around the backside of the bathroom stalls, behind bushes that grew outside the concrete wall, and spend time touching Nanda in the dark and doing things to her that all the boys wanted to do. Even Simon the Freak had put his hands on Nanda, and he was the kid who didn't even get a hug from his own mother. The boys didn't have to worry about Nanda's father and mother coming by to get her, as her parents were the neighborhood drug dealers, both of them known junkies, and most nights they were busy entertaining thugs who visited them in a black Oldsmobile with a Nevada license plate.

"Were you one of the boys who touched Nanda?"

"No, but I gave her a gift once—a little cross."

"The one you stole from Woolworth's?"

"No! It was my sister's, but she didn't want it anymore."

"Well, you still stole it if it belonged to your sister. And why did you give it to her? What did you want? Did you think nasty things about her?"

Big Boy felt his hands sweating and his heart thumping against his T-shirt. "Yes, I guess I did, but I gave her the gift because she was my friend."

"All the boys were her friends!" said Father Leo. "Don't get smart. Now, say ten Our Fathers and ten Hail Mary's as penance . . . and don't let me hear that you've been stealing again or thinking nasty thoughts about girls." Then he mumbled an absolution and raising his hand in the dim light, he blessed Big Boy and with one quick motion shut the screened panel.

THE NEXT DAY, Big Boy walked by Nanda's apartment and noticed the black Oldsmobile with the Nevada license plate parked outside on the street. He looked inside the car and noticed a girl's jacket in the back seat. Through the tinted windows, he couldn't tell if it was Nanda's.

He thought of Nanda—her soft, fleshy breasts—and felt guilty for lying to Father Leo. He had touched Nanda and had never forgotten how beautiful her skin had felt under his hand. He had kissed her too, because she had told him he could. He had looked into Nanda's dark eyes, then stared deep into the luminous pupils, shiny, as if Nanda had just shed tears, and he saw her sadness. Instinctively, he had looked up at the sky, as it seemed to him that a part of Nanda had suddenly taken flight. She had stood in front of him that Sunday night when he was still in seventh grade and she was already in eighth. She just stood there, watching his hand on her breast as if she was a mannequin, and he could have done anything he had wanted to do. Big Boy had gently smoothed back her hair and hooked the chain with the tiny silver crucifix around her neck. She had smiled at him then, and it was the first time Big Boy had seen the dimples on her cheeks. Big Boy dismissed the memory of the silver chain from his mind —the same one he had stolen from Woolworth's, another lie he had told Father Leo. The clerk had been right. He had lifted things from Woolworth's and, specifically, the silver chain that he had given to Nanda. She had been happy wearing it, and Big Boy didn't regret taking it.

NANDA WASN'T IN SCHOOL the next day, and nobody gave it a second thought; she had been absent many times, and Monday was one of her favorite days to stay home. There was talk that Nanda wouldn't be able to graduate and would have to repeat the eighth grade. Big Boy hoped she'd fail so she could be in his class, then he'd get closer to her, maybe be the one who took her behind the bathroom wall at Harmon Park.

Nanda's parents were unconcerned by her disappearance, saying she had the habit of running away to her sister's in Los Angeles and hiding out. She'd be back soon, they said. The truant officer from school stopped by and could get nothing more from them; they weren't worried, they said, she'd come back, this was normal for her. Yet, from one day to the next, Nanda didn't come back. She had disappeared, and people in the projects talked about it every day for months. The girls were glad she was gone; now they had more control over their boyfriends. Their mothers were glad to be rid of her; now their daughters wouldn't be plagued by Nanda's loose ways.

"She's probably pregnant," Atalia told Big Boy when she visited with him at juvie. "She's probably somewhere having a baby, and she'll be back after she has it."

"She never told me she'd be leaving," Big Boy said.

Atalia frowned at him. "I didn't know you were that close to her. Why should she tell you?"

"We were kind of friends," Big Boy said, squirming in his chair. Across the room, he saw one of the boys who had touched Nanda one night, pulling down her underwear, and making her cry. He looked away, remembering how she had run, with the boy holding up her underwear like a flag and laughing.

Nanda didn't come back to school, and Big Boy missed her. She had slipped her hand through his after he linked the chain with the cross around her neck and leaned on him. "You're my best friend," she had whispered to him. Big Boy remembered her voice, distant somehow, and still sensed the pressure of her hand in his, the palm of her hand warm and delicate to his touch. He had thought of Nanda every night he had spent at juvie, and now that Father Leo asked him about her, he started thinking about her all over again.

BEING ONE OF FATHER LEO'S ALTAR BOYS meant there would be many rules to follow. Big Boy had to be sure there were enough hosts for the masses he served and that the wine was ready in the chalice when the priest walked into the sacristy to serve mass. The door to the priest's closet that contained his vestments was to be unlocked, the candles on the altar had to be lit and the Bible Father Leo read from had to be placed on the altar and opened to the reading of the day.

Big Boy felt as if Father Leo could see right through him. He saw the priest kneeling down in front of a picture of the Sacred Heart of Jesus sometimes before mass with his face in his hands. He looked like he was praying, maybe listening to the voice of Jesus in his head. Big Boy felt as if the priest was watching him around the girls who came up to receive Communion during mass. He had ordered him not to think nasty thoughts, and since that time, that was all Big Boy thought about. He remembered Quincy, a black kid from juvie, who had told him all there was to know about girls and that "Real men do it to them, and don't ask any questions." Big Boy wasn't sure what "do it to them" meant but he was hoping to find out —maybe from Ernestina, one of Nanda's friends.

Big Boy had gotten into the habit of watching Ernestina at school every chance he got, noticing how her sweater plunged into a V, showing the smooth skin of her neck and, lower still to the outline of her breasts, almost identical to Nanda's. He got his courage up one day at lunch and talked to her at the drinking fountain, towering over her, even though she was one year older than he was. "Have you seen Nanda around?"

"Nah, she's gone. Her mom won't say where. I think to California." Ernestina took a drink from the fountain and the water dribbled from her lips to her chin and onto her chest. It took all of Big Boy's strength not to reach over and brush the drops of water from Ernestina's chin and kiss her. She watched him, suddenly tossing her head and laughing loud at something somebody said to her, and she walked past Big Boy like he wasn't even there.

"I'M SO PROUD OF YOU," Big Boy's mother said to him one Sunday morning at breakfast. "My own son, serving mass! Maybe some day you'll be a priest . . . yes, I want you to think about it." She picked up Big Boy's three-year-old sister, Lucy, in her arms. "Lucy can get married and have kids someday, but I want you to be a priest—a saint, like Father Leo. If it weren't for him, I don't know where we would be. He brought me a food box the other day and had the sodality help me pay the rent. I tell you, he's a saint! Now he's watching over you. Franco called him the other day to see how you're doing, and Father gave him a good report."

"Why did my probation officer call Father?" Big Boy asked.

"I told him Father Leo was as good as your own dad, and better, because he's really taking an interest in you, so he put him down as your mentor. I tell you, God's blessing us!"

Big Boy trudged to St. Anthony's that morning to serve ten-AM mass and thought of Father Leo looking through him, reading his thoughts and now he was talking to Franco.

WALKING HOME AFTER MASS, Big Boy decided to pass by Nanda's apartment. He walked past the bakery and Lowell School to get to Nanda's, all the while watching out for any of the boys who normally hung around that section of the projects. Maybe one of them would want to challenge him for coming into their territory, and then he'd have to have a good excuse or fight to get out. He saw no one. It was a spring day, the weather warm. He saw kids playing a baseball game at Harmon Park in the distance, and he caught sight of the park swings, the old rusty merry-go-round and the bathrooms, the faded walls marked up by gang graffiti, and he longed for Nanda. He longed to see her one more time, to look into her sad eyes and watch her take flight, then catch her in his arms again and fill her with kisses, slowly caressing each breast.

Big Boy saw the black Oldsmobile parked in front of Nanda's apartment, and he peered into the window, this time not spotting the girl's jacket. He saw boxes in the back seat, luggage and papers strewn on the seats.

"Hey!" yelled a man who walked out of Nanda's apartment. "What do ya think you're doing? Get away from there!" The guy was tall, over six feet, wearing a jacket in spite of the warm day. He had sunglasses on and wore a beret cocked to an angle.

"I'm not doing anything," Big Boy said. "I was just wondering, uh, if you've seen Nanda."

"And who wants to know?" asked the guy, walking leisurely up to Big Boy, lighting up a cigarette. He adjusted his beret. "Like I said, who wants to know?"

"A friend."

"She ain't got no friends—cousins, maybe, but friends?"

Big Boy felt his stomach cramp as the guy leaned next to the car, puffing on his cigarette. He stuck the cigarette in his mouth as he rolled up his sleeves to show off his tats: blue webs that climbed up his arms.

Big Boy wanted to walk away, to disappear like Nanda had, but now that he was so close to this man who had just walked out of her apartment, he was determined to get some information from him. "Are you from Las Vegas?"

"Yeah, and who wants to know?"

"Big Boy."

"You ain't that big. Nobody's big. We're all the same size. Ain't nobody can outrun a bullet." Then he laughed as he saw Big Boy's face turn pale. "Want a cigarette?"

"Nah, that's okay."

"Ah, yeah, Nanda. Now there's a girl, if you know what I mean. Now she's big . . . in all the right places." He laughed again, gruffly. "Right, Big Boy? Is that what you want? Some action?" The guy sneered, then reached into his pocket to take out his car keys. "I gotta go," he said. "Ain't got no time to be talking to big boys who are full of shit. Is Franco your probation officer?"

"Yeah. How'd you know?"

"Been on the streets all my life. Tell that son-of-a-bitch he owes me. He owes Chano, and I ain't forgot." Then he climbed into the car, and Big Boy stood watching the Oldsmobile creep down the street, thinking how Nanda would have looked sitting next to Chano, smoking a cigarette.

MONTHS WENT BY, the whole summer, and other girls joined the boys at Harmon Park—Ernestina, Yvette and a few others who were loud, and bossy, and played hard-to-get, but let themselves be caught in the end. Atalia visited Big Boy and told him to stay away from Harmon unless he wanted to get involved with narcos and floozies who did it with everybody. No matter what she told him, Harmon Park drew Big Boy like a magnet, leering at him with memories of Nanda, soft, fleshy breasts, rich warm places inside her he'd like to get to. Sometimes tears crawled down Big Boy's face late at night as he thought of Nanda disappearing like a puff of smoke, and everybody moving on with their lives as if it didn't matter at all. Maybe she was living in Las Vegas—dancing at a casino. But she was too young for that . . . or maybe she was dead. When Big Boy said the word *dead* in his mind, he flinched, as if he had been hit a blow in the face. *Dead*, her body lying out somewhere in the desert. Big Boy closed his eyes tight to block out the thought.

ON THE ANNIVERSARY of Nanda's disappearance, Father Leo called Big Boy into his office. "Stop moping around about that girl," he said nonchalantly. "I know you're trying to figure out where she is. If I were you, I'd drop it. Clean heart, remember? I think you need another confession. You're way overdue. Confession on Saturday at two PM. Be there."

"Yes, Father."

"Oh, by the way, Franco says you're almost ready to be released from probation, and I told him you are totally repented—no more shoplifting at Woolworth's. Right, Big Boy?"

"Right."

"You don't want to follow in the footsteps of Chano—you know, the guy that visits Nanda's family sometimes."

Big Boy looked up at Father Leo, surprised he knew anything about Chano. Maybe he had visited him in prison or heard his confession. Then he saw Father Leo smile broadly, as if he had just caught Big Boy sneaking a sip of wine from the chalice. He pulled open the drawer on his desk and reached in, taking out a silver chain with a small cross. He watched Big Boy closely, saw the fear in his eyes as Big Boy saw the chain he had given Nanda in Father Leo's hand. "I want you to give this to Ernestina," Father Leo said quietly, leaning close to Big Boy. "You understand, don't you?" He waited, dangling the chain in midair between them.

Then he sat back as Big Boy took the silver chain in his hand and dropped it in his pocket. "Confession on Saturday. Don't forget," Father Leo said.

Enemy Lines

Today, I'm being examined by Dr. Tim Lin—something-or-other. Can't pronounce his name—bunch of foreigners. Can't understand what he tells me either. I keep asking him to speak English, and he keeps telling me he's already doing it. Take lessons then, I tell him, can't you pronounce no better than that? I like Dr. Tim Lin though. He had a washcloth sent in before he got to the examining room so I could wash up. "Give it to Margie. She wash up, smell nice," he told the nurse, the big flabby one who always gives me problems when I make it into the emergency room. She's never explained to me why she hates me. Marion's her name, but I call her the Bar Queen because she reminds me of a bar maid I knew once back in Ohio.

There was a place—Tom's Hut or something like that, a joint I hung around until closing time. This bar maid . . . I forget her name. Betsey? Betty? I called her Breezy because she always wore dresses with big sleeves, and it looked like any breeze blowing by could fit into them. She told me one day, "You know, Margaret, times are rough. I'm getting the hell out of this joint before things get worse."

"Where to?" I asked her.

"Wherever the wind blows."

"Perfect," I told her. In my mind, I saw her flying over the horizon like Mary Poppins, the sleeves on her dress opening up like helium balloons.

Dr. Tim Lin walks in and examines my bad elbow. "Stop smoking, fool," I tell him. I can smell cigarettes on him even though he's got gum in his mouth.

He laughs. "Margie, you no lecture me, I am doctor!"

"Doctor, my ass! You're younger than my oldest kid, so don't doctor me. I'm dizzy," I tell him. "No can see. Got pain in my head over my left eye, down my shoulder."

"You been drinking?"

"Do I look drunk? I've been on the wagon for three months. Of course, I can't convince that fat slob Marion."

Marion walks in and gives me a dirty look. "She fell down the stairs over at her apartment complex," she says.

"Drinking," Dr. Tim Lin says, like he's made up his mind and nobody's gonna change it.

"Not drinking!" I yell at him. He looks over at my chart, writes something down and walks out.

"I tell you, I'm sick—can't breathe, can't walk right. I need help."

"There's nothing wrong with you, Margaret, that a few months of sobriety can't take care of." Marion's standing next to me, dingy looking. Her uniform looks threadbare.

"What's wrong, Marion? County can't afford to get you a new uniform? You look like a piece of crap."

"I don't have to put up with this!" She grabs the wall phone and calls Security.

"Who you calling? Victor on tonight? Tell him I've got the dollar I borrowed from him last week."

"You should be put in an institution and the key thrown away. Can't you see how busy we are? Do we look like we have time to baby you?"

"Baby me? You barely give me the time of day! I tell you, I'm sick. If something happens, so help me, I'll sue the whole damn lot of you . . . starting with you, you haughty bitch."

"That's it!" Marion walks out the door and into the hallway. She comes back with a cop just as I'm buttoning up my blouse.

"I know her," the cop says. "They call her Margaret Queen of Scotland. She says she's royalty."

"Yeah, and I'm the daughter of King Henry the Eighth," Marion says.

"She lives over by Third Avenue and Van Buren at one of the motels that's been taken over by street people."

"Calling me names, and we just met." I tell the cop. He's tall, a dark haired, nice-looking Mexican kid. He reminds me of my old lover Alfonso from Mexico City. Haven't seen him in years. Went back to his wife after we lived together in Nogales for two years. "Buenas noches," I tell him in perfect Spanish.

"I don't speak Spanish," he says.

"What a shame. You look like you do. I've known lots of people from Mexico—nice people, not like that creature over there. "

"What a mouth! Nothing but trouble with her. She's a steady customer. Can't get enough of us," Marion tells the cop.

"Let me handle it." The cop nods his head at Marion, and she stomps out.

"Sore loser."

"Come on, Margaret, don't make things hard for yourself. I'll walk you outside. You can sit by the curb for a while, or I'll drive you home. How's that?" He grabs my canvas bag and hands it to me, then helps me off the examining table. My knees are wobbly, and he notices.

"Lean on me, Margaret. It's okay."

"Isn't there a song called, *Lean on Me*? I haven't heard that in years. If only I could lean on people sometimes."

We're walking out slow; there're people wall-to-wall. I can't resist the temptation to stick out my tongue at Marion as we pass her in the hall. She turns her face away, as if she hasn't seen me.

"Okay, Margaret, let up on her. I thought you were royalty."

"Yeah, you're right. Why waste my strength? She's a peon."

I see a woman puking in a bag. She's sitting up on an examining table, her head cocked at a strange angle. A man up against the wall looks dead, the white sheet stopping at his chin. He's perfectly still, his face ashen gray. A young woman is holding an older woman, probably her mother. The older woman is crying, lamenting, "Why, why?" Family members are standing up against the wall outside the examining rooms. Two-way radios sound up and down the hall, cops and paramedics talking to each other. One man is brought in on a stretcher, and two paramedics exchange a joke as they ease the man onto a hospital bed. "How many times can a sinner knock on Heaven's door?" I don't hear the answer, only the two men laughing.

Two small boys are playing by the automatic door, making it open and shut over and over again. One little girl is throwing peanuts at the two boys. I know this drives Marion crazy, and it makes me smile.

"Something funny?"

"Look at this place. Ever heard of the movie *One Flew over the Cuckoo's Nest*? This is it—the pits. I'm telling you, my father would have sued everybody in the place."

"Was your father an attorney?"

"No. He was an interested citizen. Really he was a rebel, a Hell's Angel. He sued for everything. One time he sued one of my teachers for not giving me a pencil at school. After that, I got pencils every week."

"I'm Miguel," he says.

"Miguel? But you don't speak Spanish!"

He pats my arm. "I know. Maybe you can teach me."

I like the kid. I press closer to him. His body is all muscle; mine feels like Jell-O. I stagger a bit, stopping to balance my bag.

"Give me your bag, Margaret. I'll carry it."

We reach the automatic door, exit and walk between the two little boys, stepping over stray peanuts. The Mexican cop tells the boys to pick up the peanuts or he'll arrest them. He laughs, and they run away.

The night air hits me like a punch between the eyes. It's late February, a crisp, moonless night. It's been raining off and on. The streets are wet, the asphalt slick with oil. I smell car exhaust, grease. I wipe grime off my face. Already I feel dirty, instantly nauseated. I take a deep breath to get oxygen to my brain, and the nausea gets worse.

"I can drive you home, Margaret. You don't live too far away. We'll consider it a date."

I smile at the kid and keep walking. I don't have the energy to say anything.

Streetlights are hazy, nebulous, as we walk out. It reminds me of streets I saw in London when I was a kid. "This looks like London."

"Phoenix looks like London? That's the first time I've heard that. When were you in London?"

"Ages ago. I was only four. My grandmother lived there."

"So you *are* royalty." He pats my hand.

I'm confused and don't know which way is north or if I live up or down on Van Buren Street. I want to tell the Mexican cop my address, but can't make it out in my mind.

"Go by Sal's Diner. Andrea should be working there. She'll give you my address."

"Sal's has been closed for ten years, Margaret. Did you forget? It's been sold, but nobody knows to whom. Don't worry . . . I got your address. Wasn't Andrea the waitress? I met her once."

"I've known her for years. Her daughter Joanna too, except Joanna went off to college. Good people. Andrea helped me hundreds of times, I can tell you that."

There's Joanna in my mind, all dressed up in her eighth-grade graduation dress with the white lacy top—all grown up, her hair done up in baby's breath. She must have come home by now, but where did she go? There's a flash of something white at the edge of my vision, then it's gone. I'm grateful for the Mexican kid. He's a cop but he's got heart. He lets me sit up front, instead of in the back

I WAKE UP EARLY. "Friday," I say to myself and don't know why I said it.

I hear Gertie next door. He's got the faucet on, starting coffee. He's a woman turned man. Done the operation on himself four years ago. Said he missed getting a penis, so he put one in. "No matter," he says, "the artificial one fits just right." Once in a while he has company over, usually another woman but sometimes a man; he's not particular. I asked why he didn't change his name to Guthrie or Gary, but he says what for? Legal documents call him Gertrude no matter what he says.

I can tap on the wall, get his attention if I want to, but don't have the strength to pick up my arm. Not drinking, and I'm wasted. Suddenly, I want a drink but have none in the apartment. My bladder feels full thinking about drinking. I have to get up . . . no more accidents. I hate the smell, and then there's the rash, and everything gets raw, red. I get up and try to stand. That bastard Tim Lin. He could have done something for me, but he's too busy sneaking around smoking, acting innocent, like he obeys all the rules. I know sly when I see it. Piss on Marion, too. She'll get hers someday. She'll get old. It catches up to everybody. Energetic was my middle name.

Can't stand, so I crawl on all fours to the bathroom. Nobody's watching. Gertie can't hear me crawling around, although sometimes he's heard me fall. Then he comes in . . . blustering is what I call it. He's little, 'cause underneath it all, he's a woman. I can make out breasts, but don't tell him, 'cause he's cried before, saying his operation was a failure. He's helped me before, "putting muscle in it," he says, fussing and finally raising me up to where I can stand and walk on my own. "Get to the hospital," he says, and I tell him, "Get lost! Can't you see what happens to people like me when we ask for help? We wait so long, we about die just waiting, and who needs that. Especially when I could die just as easily in my own bed." I've let Gertie help me take a bath. He's a woman, after all, so I have nothing to fear. There's no attraction, and at my age, I wouldn't care anyway.

Can't remember falling asleep, but I guess it happened. Someone's at the door. The Mexican cop? Sun coming in through the broken blinds—hard, white—and I hate it. No appetite. Gertie hasn't come over to check. Knocking doesn't stop. "Get the hell out!" I tell whoever it is.

"Mrs. Claybourne? I'm from the Arizona State Dependents Office. Open the door, please."

"Ain't got time. I'm busy!"

"I have to make a welfare check. If you won't open, I'll get the manager."

I think of the screwball who's the manager. Vicious ball 'a hair is what I call him. Hairy like a monkey, staring into every crook and cranny, spraying for cockroaches, neutralizing the bathroom. Shit, he don't live here. What does he care?

"Get the key. It's under the mat." I sit up in bed, try to perk up. No telling what he'll say—maybe commit me someplace. Can't trust anybody from the State. Guy walks in: nice shirt even though it's pink; no tie; pants pressed, creases down the middle; no briefcase; pad in hand. Looks around, up, down, eyes traveling to me.

"Are you ill, Mrs. Claybourne?"

"Oh, God, boy, what does it look like?" He goes to the sink, pours a glass of water for me, sits on a chair and fixes the rim of the glass at my mouth. The glass collides with my teeth as I take a drink.

"Take a drink. Take a sip, Mrs. Claybourne," he says like he's talking to a kid. The water feels good down my throat. I'm thirsty and ask him for more. He makes another trip to the sink, another glass. Same thing . . . fits it up to my lips, collides with my teeth. Another trip to the sink, and he wets a paper towel, folds it up, puts it over my forehead. He turns on the fan, opens up the window, just a bit. "Better?" he asks me.

"Yeah, better."

He's got cologne on. I notice his face for the first time—a dead ringer for Alvin, dead ringer. Same jaw line, soft, barely a chin, clean-shaven. Eyes gray that turn brown. Nose off center, lips thick, ending in creases. "Alvin?"

"No, ma'm. I'm Troy Hallerman. Who's Alvin?"

"My sweetheart." He smiles, and he's Alvin, pretending, paying me a visit in my old age. He was always like that—playing pranks, slinging me over his shoulder, kidnapping me away from my father, Mom lying sick in bed. Us ditching class, over by Ol' Barter's Belt, where there was a lake. The lake was shiny, gray, not deep unless you got in the middle, but we never did. We stayed on the shore, stroking each other, his fingers tangled in my hair. He was one for caressing, toes crawling up my leg. Fitting himself over my body, shyly at first, then urgently. Giving in to him with birds chirping overhead, so happy for us young lovers, they had to sing. Everything was singing, and the sun warm overhead.

"Alvin, you coming for me?"

"Where do you want to go, Mrs. Claybourne?"

"Ol' Barter's Belt."

"Mrs. Claybourne, I think you're hallucinating. I need to call an ambulance."

"Don't tell my dad. You know he'll get mad. Hated you, so he sent you away! It wasn't me that wanted it that way. You remember, don't you, Alvin? The secret between you and me? It was all the same to me. Forgive me. I know you wanted to keep that baby! You pined after that baby, but I said no. It was me who gave it up. Alvin, did you hear me? Quit blaming yourself after all these years, for God's sake! Stop looking at me like that. We both done it all wrong."

"Mrs. Claybourne, I'm getting help for you. I can't understand what you're saying."

White light starts at the corner of my eye, spreads, splits in two, sprinkles me with confetti. "There's a party going on. Alvin's giving me a party, and I didn't know it was my birthday."

"Mrs. Claybourne, I'm taking your pulse. Hold still, please. Breathe slow. Don't force yourself."

Gertie's in the room. I smell his perfume. He's just showered. "Alvin's here," I tell him. "Come all the way from Ohio to pick me up."

Gertie's face is all smiles, tears. He's close and gentle, not blustering this time.

"Alvin from Ohio?"

"My sweetheart. We were sixteen."

"Get her some help. Can't you see what's happening?" says Gertie.

My hands get cold, stomach hard—a big cramp I can't get rid of. Light breaks overhead, confetti; the party's still going on. "Alvin's got a party for me, Gertie."

Gertie doesn't say anything.

I'm talking in my head, but it doesn't reach my lips. "Water," I say, but no one hears.

Alvin's got his hand to my throat. "Stop it," I tell him. "You're hurting me. Be gentle, or I'll tell."

"Nobody's gonna hurt you, Mrs. Claybourne."

Mrs. Claybourne's my mother, for God's sake, not me. From Scotland, the Highlands, that's where she's from. Dirt poor, got kicked off her land, made her way over enemy lines with over 200 clan members, to Connecticut, Pennsylvania, Ohio. Lost her crown, that's what she said to me and Alvin. Used to be royalty, owned half the Highlands, then it was gone. Nobody believed me—not one soul except Alvin. I gave him the cross, all gold, the only thing my mother had left, to make up for the baby. The cross for the baby. God forgive me!

White light spreading, Alvin playing games, thumbs stuck in my throat. "How long can you hold your breath?" so I start to play. Hold it, Margie, hold it for Alvin. The more I hold it, the more he laughs. It makes him happy, so I do it again. He gets closer. Suddenly, I know I gotta cross enemy lines to get to him, like my mother did to get to America. She did; it so can I. White confetti falling all around me like snow, then a gentle kiss from Alvin.

Gertie's far away, his face, long and tired, his eyes red. "Margie, hang on!"

"To what?" I ask him. "I gotta cross enemy lines, gotta get to Alvin. There's things undone—the boy we lost. God watching us."

One hour later, paramedics arrive, the same ones at the emergency room, joking, to pick up Margaret's body. "One more stiff," they say, "Thank God she doesn't weigh much. God, what a mess these people live in. The County should be sued for not providing." They're hurrying, planning their next meal at the Chinese South Buffet. They're doing a favor for the County. The morgue people are tied up—too many people dying all at once, and now this. For sure, they'll be late for lunch, and who knows if they'll get to eat before their shift is over.

TROY HALLERMAN STUCK IN HIS CHAIR AT WORK, computer on, writing up the facts. *Margaret Claybourne, alias Margaret Queen of Scotland, expired at 3:25 this afternoon, February 28, 2000. Obviously hallucinating, identifying me as Alvin, past sweetheart from Ohio. Paramedics were called at 2:53. Expired before they arrived. Neighbor, Gertrude Osborn, related Margaret Claybourne had been in poor health for months and was unable to get good medical care. Related he planned to sue the emergency crew at Phoenix Memorial Hospital for not providing the atten-*

tion she needed. No family members identified. To be buried in County plot.

Troy Hallerman, adopted son of Karen and Thomas Hallerman of Oakdale, Ohio, thirty miles outside of Barter's Belt sighs, yawns. He's just witnessed his first death. Not as bad as he thought it would be.